Only The Lonely

Susan Gabriel

ISBN 978-0-9802246-6-5

Published 2010 Republished 2015
Published by Black Velvet Seductions Publishing

Only the Lonely Copyright 2010 Susan Gabriel
Cover design Copyright 2015 R. J. Savage

Published 2015
Printed by Black Velvet Seductions Publishing
A division of Savage Publications

Visit us at:
www.blackvelvetseductions.com

Deep in the heart of Summer, sweet is life to me still,
But my heart is a lonely hunter, that hunts on a lonely hill.
William Sharp

Susan Gabriel

Only The Lonely

"Live in three...two...one." The countdown reverberated through her headphones, triggering ritual actions that were so automatic she scarcely noticed performing them: a quick sip of tepid coffee, an imperceptible uptake of heart rate and a straightening of her spine as she leaned into the microphone.

The studio was her domain; familiar and empowering. She could say whatever she wanted, minus a few words prohibited by the FCC. The time slot was perfect, too. Conversing with her faceless friends and followers allowed her to forget about the empty spaces in her life and in her bed, but tonight the void coursed through her veins with a prickly agitation.

Her lips brushed the cold steel, as the timbre of her voice made love to the airwaves.

"Hello, darkness, my old friend. I've come to talk with you again. You're listening to KJZM late night talk radio. I'm your host, Summer Solstice, and this is: Only the Lonely. We have about an hour and a half remaining in tonight's show. I'm reaching out to touch all of the lonely people - you know who you are - so call and tell me your story. Are you sighing in the solitude of a darkened room, like some long-forgotten ghost trying to make contact with the human world? Are you in bed, wrapped in the warmth of a dependable blanket instead of in the protective arms of a lover? I want you to use your finger and push my buttons. You know what I'm talking about, St. Louis - I crave to learn every last detail of what landed you in the mournful condition that you now find yourself in. Our phone lines are open, and we'll be taking our next caller right after a few words from Naughty by Night Oils and Unguents; creator of the most requested brand of lubricant; Snake-eye and Slick."

Summer removed her headphones and shook her ash blonde hair

into place. The leather of the studio chair creaked like a rusty hinge as she leaned back and propped her black-stockinged legs on the console.

Glancing at the clock, weariness settled over her. It had been a long night of characterless callers, full of insipid platitudes. No one wanted to admit how truly miserable they were, so they justified it with clichéd references about the fortitude-building benefits of solitude.

Being alone was sometimes a very good thing; being lonely always sucked. After doing this gig for so many years, Summer sensed that it had begun to take its toll. Cynicism was wrapping its roots around her soul. So many sad stories…so many miserable lives…so much misery and too few solutions.

"Hey, Summer, you're sounding great tonight." A voice echoed from behind the glass of the control room.

Summer peered past the soundproof glass into the blue light of the control room. *Reliable Melody…always good for an encouraging comment.* Summer grinned at her production assistant, who was smiling and signaling the 'thumbs up' sign. At least Summer thought that she was smiling. It might have been the light glinting off of one of her lip piercings.

Summer knew she couldn't do this show without Melody. She and Melody had been a team for over twelve years - moving from one radio market to the next, like a pair of gypsies, until finally landing at KJZM. Now they hosted the top Arbitron rated late night show in the Midwest market.

Closer than sisters, they knew and kept each other's secrets. They truly were the oddest of pairs, Summer thought. Even when she stretched herself to her full five foot four inches, she was dwarfed by Melody, who towered nearly five foot ten in her combat boots. Summer frequently wore her hair twisted carelessly around a number two pencil at the nape of her neck, preferring the classic look of a simple pencil skirt, a couture blouse and a stylish pair of pumps, while Melody was all leather and metal, studs and tats.

Melody was in-your-face brash sensuality. She was tough as nails, but with the heart of a lion.

Summer couldn't afford such self-expression. As the front woman for their team, she needed to be taken seriously. She consciously chose to tone down her own sexuality for a more buttoned-up, naughty school teacher appearance.

"Who's cued up on the lines?" Summer asked, while reaching for her coffee mug.

"Let's see, I have Jerry, of course, on line one," replied Melody, her tongue ring softly clacking against her teeth as she spoke.

Jerry...Summer banged her head once softly on the back of her chair. She was in no mood for Jerry's antics tonight, but if she didn't take his call, he would only harass Melody, whining and pleading that he had to get through tonight, claiming falsely that it was a matter of life and death.

"There's a Bob from Creve Couer on line two, and Lucien from Lafayette Square on three. He sounds very cute, and has a super sexy French accent."

"Well, I suppose we should get Jerry over with for the night, so put him through first." Summer winced. "Save Lucien from Lafayette Square for last."

"OK, Summer. Your lead-in ad copy is lying on the console," directed Melody, her tattooed hands throwing switches in the sound booth. "I'm cuing the jingle."

Augustus Gloop, Augustus Gloop, droned the jingle, *don't be a Sexual Nincompoop!*

Pressing her lips closely to the microphone, Summer recited, "Augustus Gloop condoms wants to remind you that, the next time you stop by the candy store, or pay a visit to the chocolate factory, remember to wrap your Willie Wonka in an Augustus Gloop condom -now in two new flavors; blueberry and ever-lasting-gob-stopper."

Summer shook her head and rolled her eyes. Lord, what a girl had to do to make a living. Who thinks up this shit, she wondered. It was the curse of the late-night time slot - adult advertising that would have every prude in a hundred mile radius picketing the station if they aired during regular hours.

Summer smoothly transitioned into a call. "Hello, caller," she cooed. "Tell me why you're lonely tonight."

"Hi, Summer, it's Jerry, remember me?" squeaked the voice on the line.

She wasn't up for playing his game. Her feet hurt, her stomach was empty and she needed a smoke.

"Let's see...now let me think... Jerry... Jerry... hmmm... Oh wait! Are you the Jerry that calls me every single night and says, 'Hi Summer, it's Jerry, remember me?' That Jerry - is that the one?" Summer honestly did not know what to do with Jerry. On the one hand, his pervy little calls could be as annoying as sand in your pants. On the other hand, he was peculiarly popular with her listeners. He even had his own fan club of sorts. Jerry never missed an opportunity to hitch his wagon to Summer's star, frequently showing up at appearances and live remotes.

Summer often bantered with Jerry and egged him on in the name of ratings, but tonight she found the sound of his nasally voice beyond irritating.

"Oh, you remember me then?"

What a dork.

"Yes, Jerry, I remember you. What's on your mind tonight?" Summer glanced at Melody, curling her lip in an exaggerated sneer. Melody responded with a full body shiver.

"What color underwear are you wearing?"

Oh, Christ. How many ways and how many times can I answer that question from him? At least once a week, he used the underwear question as his opener...or maybe it was his erection trigger. Either way, he was a bore.

"Oh, now there's a fresh one. Who did you borrow that from Jerry? Noah?"

Summer wanted to put an end to this ridiculousness once and for all. She enjoyed healthy banter as much as the next gal, but she was fed up, and she bet that her listeners were too. She could almost hear her numbers tanking as she spoke.

"See, the problem here is, Jerry - when you call me every night, eventually you are going to run out of interesting new ways to talk dirty to me, so that's when you are forced to resurrect the same lines that didn't work for you 'back in the day' when you were just a fledging pervert, trying out your wings by pestering the Prom Queen of your high school."

Oh, this felt good. Time to wake up those sleepy listeners. If Jerry thinks he can embarrass me and put me on the spot, I'll just have to teach him who runs this show.

For a moment, every creep that had ever made a power play on her swam through her mind...the little nerd at the donut shop who told her with a wink that he had filled an éclair especially for her...the squirrelly little mongoose of a shoe salesman who ran his hand up her skirt, and a thousand other nameless douche bags that got off on seeing her squirm. Enough was enough.

"Let's face facts. We both know, Jerry, that you are forty-seven years old and still beating the bishop in your mother's basement." Summer spit the retort in a single breath.

"I, um…" Jerry mumbled.

Summer leaned closer to the mike. "Listen very closely, Jerry-- "

"Yeah, Summer, I…"

"Ah-ah! No talking, Jerry, just listening." Summer glanced in Melody's direction. Melody curled her fingers into the "rock-on" gesture.

"Jerry, you will never, I repeat never, have the privilege of knowing the color, type, brand or cut of my underwear. Never, ever. I don't want to have to screen out your calls, Jerry. Sometimes you aren't so bad to talk to. But do the city a favor and either stay on your meds, or stay off the phone."

Her manicured finger decisively pressed a small white button, effectively ending the call.

It felt satisfying. Just like that, *bam*, no Jerry.

"Hello…hello…aw, so sorry, it looks like Jerry was disconnected." Summer snickered.

"We'll just have to go to our next caller; Bob, from Creve Couer." She consciously sweetened her tone of voice. "Hello Bob."

"Hello, Summer," croaked Bob.

"Bob, tell our listeners what made you the lonely person you are today." "Well, Summer. I wasn't always lonely." His voice cracked with an odd desperation. "I used to have a family. I even had a dog - a beagle. That was a great dog. I lost everything; my wife, my kids, and my dog. There's something wrong with me. I don't know what it is…"

Why do we always blame ourselves when things turn to shit? Summer wondered.

"Now wait, Bob. Perhaps it isn't your fault. It does take two to tango. You say that there is something wrong with you. What do you think that something might be?"

Bob took in a sharp breath, held it for a moment and then slowly exhaled. "I'm not well, Summer. I see things. Things that are there, but aren't there."

"Hallucinations, Bob? Like big pink elephants and monsters under the bed?" *This one might be above my pay grade*, thought Summer.

"Not exactly, but sort of…at least the monster part. I see vampires."

Summer's heart skipped a beat. Her eyes darted to the control booth, but Melody wasn't paying attention. Pursing her lips, she prodded, "I'm listening, Bob. Go on."

"I know that there's no such thing, but it doesn't stop me from seeing them - everywhere."

Summer reached for her cold coffee, trying to drown away the turmoil that began to swirl in her stomach.

"Summer," he went on. "I see them everywhere. Nobody else sees 'em. When I point them out, other people just see a regular person, but I don't, Summer - I see a vampire!"

Could Bob from Creve Coeur be a fellow Perceiver? No wonder his wife and kids left him. Poor bastard. His shrink probably had him on cures that were worse than the disease.

Summer had found out personally that the first step in coming to grips with being a Perceiver was assurance that you aren't insane, and that vampires are a fact of life. Once that sinks into your brain, then you have a whole new set of issues to deal with. It's an altered reality. The world is turned upside down. Death, life, good, evil, God, or no God... nothing is as it was. No black, no white, only varying shades of gray.

But first comes assurance.

Cautiously, Summer opened the subject. "I don't know about everyone, Bob, but I believe in vampires."

Simply knowing that another person believes you can do wonders. If Bob truly was a Perceiver, and he wasn't sick or a nutbag, he needed to know that. In fact, there was nothing wrong with him that a few vodka tonics wouldn't cure. The truth be told, he should be celebrating his ability. St. Louis was an antique city where creatures of the night abounded in a limitless supply. Better to perceive than not to perceive.

"You do?" he asked.

"Yes, Bob, I do believe in vampires. I do because I, too, can see vampires." Summer tried to sound cheerful and matter-of-fact. Act like it's all much ado about nothing. As easy as saying that you see butterflies in spring. "I'll bet you didn't know that, but it's true. I can spot 'em a mile away.

That is, when they choose to make themselves visible. I haven't become quite skilled enough to see them when they don't want to be seen."

She probably should be keeping her mouth shut. St. Louis could also be a dangerous place for an outed Perceiver. She knew Vamps didn't want to be seen; they wanted to blend.

However, it was the very wee hours of the morning, and Summer figured the vamps were drinking their last-call Bloody Mary right about now. She needed to help this guy out in some small way…give him some advice to calm his fears without giving away too much of herself.

"Listen to me, Bob. Vampires are real…as real as you or me. You are not cuckoo. You are not delusional. You are just different, and that's not a bad thing. So take heart, and take my advice. Keep your eyes open and your mouth shut, or you are going to end up in the psych ward of St John's Mercy Hospital."

Melody tilted her head, giving Summer a "what the fuck" look.

Summer gave a "what the fuck, it's true" shrug of her shoulders. Melody followed that by slicing her finger across her throat in a warning, her eyes bulging out like a bush baby.

Melody was mothering her again. Summer knew that, behind that tough exterior, lay a frustrated Jewish nana. Melody was probably right. Talking about her ability over the air was not the best idea she had ever had. Damn, wouldn't this night ever be over with? She was bone-tired and not thinking clearly. Melody held up a typed page pointing at it, indicating that it was time for a commercial break.

Thank God, a convenient way to get off of this subject.

Summer smoothly segued. "But, Bob, enough about you; let's talk about me, and how much I love Frigamajig Adult Toys. As my listeners know, I only endorse and rate the Frigamajig toys that I have personally tested on myself or others, and I want to introduce you to the newest addition to Frigamajig's Small and Discreet line: The Pocket Porpoise."

Gotta love the perks of this job, she thought with a sly smile, remembering her own little porpoise with a purpose in her bedside drawer.

"The Pocket Porpoise is the perfect companion for coast to coast flights. You will find that it is barely audible above the roar of the jet engines. I give this product four out of five Gloryholes. It didn't rate a full five Gloryholes because of battery life - they burned out within a few short days, so be sure to keep extra double As on hand.
The Pocket Porpoise - pick it up at any Frigamajig Adult Toy location."

Pushing her chair away from the console, she spun it around once and drummed her palms on the desk in a finale.

She brushed a stray strand of hair from her face. It had been a long weird night and she was ready to wrap it up. An hour left in the show, and only one blinking line. The rain must have lulled everyone to sleep. Perhaps the next caller would provide some amusement.

Summer didn't get many calls from Lafayette Square. It was a desirable neighborhood of posh restored town homes that was studded with strategically placed manicured green spaces - an oasis amid the smoke-belching factories of the city.

Summer depressed the lone lighted button which connected her to her lone, lonely caller.

"Lucien from Lafayette Square is on the line. Lucien, I didn't think the privileged people in Lafayette Square were ever lonely. Isn't it just a party twenty-four seven up there?"

Summer grudgingly acknowledged to herself that she had often passed by the stately old homes, their lamplight glittering from the hand blown glass windows, and secretly wished that she could be part of it all. The sad truth of the matter was that she could live a dozen lifetimes and still not be able to afford the luxury of the Square.

She bit her tongue and resolved to stop acting like such an envious bitch.

"But I'm being presumptuous and unfair. I'm sure that privileged people get lonely. Everyone is lonely sometime. Are you lonesome tonight, Lucien from Lafayette Square?"

"It seems as if I have been lonely for centuries."

The voice on the line was heart-rendingly forlorn. Its tone conveyed the sorrow of certainty that whatever circumstances had caused its distress would never change, never look brighter, but instead would remain exactly as they were until the day he died. It was a type of poignant gloom that chilled Summer to the marrow of her bones.

"Oh, I'm sure it couldn't have been actual centuries. That's a little dramatic," she joked, trying to lighten the mood. "I thi—"

His voice broke in, melodious with richly rounded tones and a strong, yet not thick, accent that made every word sound like poetry.

"No, it has. It has been centuries," Lucien corrected. "Since, oh, 1789... so, let's see...1789, 1889, 1989, two thousand eighty-ni—oh, alright, two and a quarter centuries. Is my math correct?"

For the first time in her loquacious life, Summer was rendered mute. Was this guy pulling her leg? Summer had a subtle suspicion that he wasn't. She could smell bullshit like a fart in an elevator, and this didn't reek of a lie.

"Summer, are you there?" Lucien asked, his voice disturbingly haunting. Blinking her eyes, Summer straightened her spine, as if roused from a daydream. "Yes, yes, I'm here."

"Summer, imagine how it might feel if you knew that you were going to live forever - always remaining in the shadows, never capable of forming lasting relationships. You have lifetimes of love to share, but know that love will forever and ever remain unrequited. So, all you see unfolding in your future is oceans of loneliness." The hypnotic quality of his voice drew Summer in and for a small moment she felt a strange emptiness of spirit, as if she were only a casual and constant observer of life; detached from all emotion, a wandering specter amid the toils and tears of humanity.

The soothing notes of the caller's voice played on. "It's a strange suffering, knowing with certainty that, year after year, century after century, there is nothing but solitude stretching out from here to eternity."

A stinging began to burn behind Summer's eyes. Somehow, the caller had awakened her to the reality of her own solitude. She had always just assumed that one day she would find the right person to share her life. But what if there was no fairy tale ending for her? Would there be a day when, like Lucien, she would resign herself to the realization that she was, and always would be utterly alone? Summer choked back a lump in her throat.

What the heck was going on? Surely he was pulling her leg. None of this could be true, yet, without a doubt, she felt that it was. His voice, his words, they were like glistening ribbons of spider silk weaving through her brain, and drawing her ever deeper into his world.

No one was meant to walk a lifetime of solitary confinement, let alone dozens of lifetimes. She didn't have a clue what to say next. Whenever her friends needed cheering up, they called on good old Summer, who was always ready with a lighthearted approach. Comfort wasn't her shtick, nor was it her occupation. Glibness was her claim to fame.

"That's pretty heavy stuff, Lucien. But, hey, no one lives forever, so that's a plus." She knew it was a poor attempt at a joke and cringed even as the words left her mouth.

"Well, one can hope," the caller replied with sly sarcasm. "I heard your previous call, Summer and I am wondering, can you truly see vampires? If a person passed you on the street, could you tell if they were a vampire?"

Summer did not want to tackle that subject again -especially with this caller. Her intuition told her to proceed with caution.

"Lucien, if you are as old as you say you are, then you should have learned by now not to believe everything that you hear." "Of course. I was just hoping that we might have some special ability in common. I have an interesting parlor trick that I like to perform. I can look at people and discern what they have been drinking. Jack Daniels for this one, Coors Light for that one, and you, for instance, you drink Cutty Sark on the rocks - doubles."

A stinging shock rippled up Summer's spine, causing her to snatch her hand away from the microphone. Her mind felt muddy and confused. The radio business has a term for what happened next: Dead Air.

Her eyes darted back and forth over the pulsing red and green lights of the soundboard. She tried frantically to recall if she had met this man before. Was his voice familiar? Surely she would have remembered him.

Her face was on billboards and buses all over town. He could have recognized her any number of places ordering her favorite drink. Maybe she should think about getting a bodyguard. The notion made her shiver.

An insistent rapping reverberating on the glass of the sound booth returned Summer to her senses.

Crap, she'd been sitting there like a mute. For how long? She scrambled to shake the confusion from her head. Her reflection on the control room glass displayed the panicked look on her face.

Melody was whipping her index finger in rapid, tight circles, signaling for her to wrap it up.

"I'm sorry, but it's time to go to a commercial break, so…" Summer tentatively recovered.

"One more thing, Summer," Lucien interrupted. "Your top button is undone." The floating melody of words caressed her ears and glided through her brain, shattering in a million pieces with the stereophonic buzz of a dial tone.

Melody quickly cued a commercial for Rex Railback's Herbal Male Enhancers. Summer removed her headphones. Glancing downward, she saw that her top button was open, exposing a small bit of white lace. Hairs prickled on the back of her neck with the eerie suspicion that she was being watched. She twisted her chair in the direction of the lone window of the studio. The notion that anyone could see her was ridiculous; the studio was on the fifth floor and looked out upon the blankness of a brick wall across the alleyway.

She re-buttoned her blouse, her trembling fingers betraying her struggle to regain composure.

"Hey, are you okay?" Melody's voice called out over the intercom.

Shit, she had to get a grip. She was feeling a bit unhinged, and oddly emotional, as if she didn't know whether she wanted to laugh or cry. And that voice...that voice. Summer tried to recall it, but it kept drifting just out of reach, like a long-forgotten dream. She'd been too long without the comfort of a cigarette and some fresh air.

Gathering her things, Summer waved her hand, nodding her head. "I'm fine, I'm fine. You know what, Melody? Put on something canned for a while, I need a smoke, maybe two."

"What do you want me to air?"

Summer didn't give a fisherman's fuck what she aired. She wanted to separate herself from that last call as fast as her legs could carry her.

"I don't give a shit. Put on the Best of Jerry." Summer flung her arms wide, palms upturned. "Whatever, Melody...just put on anything."

Summer felt a momentary pang of regret. She didn't like the churlish way she sounded just now, snapping at Melody.

"Sounds like somebody just let a caller get the best of her," Melody grumbled under her breath.

Smoke and Mirrors

Claustrophobia strangled her with a suffocating embrace. The walls grew closer, squeezing the stale oxygen from the narrow hallway. Driven to fill her lungs with long gulps of fresh air, Summer jogged down five flights of metal stairs; the echo of her footsteps filled the stairwell with a metallic, booming clatter which assaulted her ears like the tolling of an out-of-tune bell.

What she needed most right now was a few moments of solitude, and the comforting ritual of feeding her nicotine addiction.

Lucien…the mere recollection of his name and her heart began to race. Like a song that repeats and repeats in your head, the beautiful melody of his voice floated hauntingly through her mind. Making her way to the exit door, she tried to piece together the moments of their brief conversation - the business about him being lonely for centuries and the other clever parlor tricks he had played on her. Playing! Yes, that's exactly what he had been doing. He had been playing her - messing with her head like a master manipulator of minds.

He sounded beautiful and tragically sad, and she had fallen for it hook, line and sinker. She wanted to kick her own ass for being suckered into his shell game like some just-off-the-turnip-truck rube.

Nice job of letting your imagination get the better of you, she thought, as she pushed the security bar on the back exit. Swinging the door wide, she filled her lungs with the moist air of the damp alleyway. Bracing her back against the heavy steel door to hold it open, she surveyed the darkened path, which was as empty as a poor man's pocket. It had rained earlier and now the street shimmered with oily pools of water that somehow appeared luminously bewitching in the moonlight; quite opposite of the dreary pot-holed cement sprawl which it actually was.

She struck a match and lit a Marlboro Light. The yellow flame cast an inky, exaggerated shadow of her figure on the wet pavement.

It's funny, she thought, *how one thing is so dreadful in the harsh glare of day, yet enchantingly beautiful in the light of the moon.*

"Like this city for instance, when you view it from a very high place." The whisper came from everywhere and nowhere simultaneously. For a split second, Summer thought she felt a warm rush of breath in her ear, accompanying the man's murmured voice.

She pivoted on her toes, adrenaline coursing through her veins, her eyesight and hearing as keen as an eagle, as she searched for the source of the voice.

Across the alley, she spied a young man leaning idly against the brick wall, a cigarette pinched between his fingers, European style. He made no move toward her, only offering the smallest wave of hello with his hand. Summer narrowed her eyes, attempting to bring his face into focus in the dim light, but it remained obscured in shadow. She, on the other hand, realized she was fully illuminated by the light pouring through the open doorway.

How strange she hadn't heard him approach or noticed him when she had stepped outside. Dropping her gaze towards the ground, why she hadn't detected him became clear. In the glistening, rain-filled pothole which separated them, he cast no reflection, except for the tell-tale bluish soul-flame which floated above his unseen body.

He was a vampire—a vampire smoking a cigarette.

Swallowing the stone in her throat, she talked herself down by mentally issuing orders to play it cool, even though she felt anything but. Her whole life, she'd longed to meet one of these creatures in person, and now one simply shows up smoking a cigarette and making casual conversation. Digging in her heels, she willed herself to remain rooted. She would not allow fear to chase her away from this once-in-a-lifetime occasion.

There is nothing to fear, she told herself even as she leaned harder against the exit door, and placed one foot inside of the building. She eased her hand to the door lever which pressed against her lower back, ready to pull it closed behind her in the event a hasty retreat might be required.

"In the glare of day, the city is dirty and belching clouds of toxic waste into the sky." He paused to drag on his cigarette, flaring it with a red-orange glow, briefly illuminating the lower half of his face. "But at night, when the lights of the city are sparkling from the windows of the high-rises, and the radiance of the moon is reflected in the churning currents of the Mississippi; now that's magic, pure magic."

Even as he spoke in softened tones, Summer detected a charming, almost musical accent. The cadence of his speech was like a long-forgotten lullaby spilling from his lips, which were not pale as she knew his flesh must be, but full and blushing with the vigor of youth.

He flicked his cigarette into the black puddle. It sizzled briefly before surrendering its fire to the water.

"It's all in the perspective, you know, mon petite."

Mon petite? Ah, of course, the accent was French; but not the thick, indecipherable accent of a recent immigrant, instead one that comes after many years of acclimation to the English language. The vampire didn't merely speak English; he purred it. Just like…no, *exactly* like her caller.

This night was getting freakier by the minute. Certainly, this was no coincidence. Lucien of Lafayette Square and the vampire standing before her must be one and the same.

She wondered what his purpose might be, and whether it was benign or treacherous. He'd sought her out for a reason, and, despite the feeling that there was a hamster ball rolling around in her stomach, she wanted desperately to know what he wanted.

The vampire withdrew a cigarette pack from his shirt pocket, and from across the narrow alleyway, he stretched out his arm and offered her one.

"Thanks, but I already have one," Summer deferred, displaying what was left of her cancer stick. She wouldn't have taken one, even if she wanted - candy from strangers and all. Clinging to the semi-safety of the doorway, she refused to be so easily lured from its false sense of security, although she was certain that if he chose, he could be on top of her faster than she could blink.

He tapped a single cigarette from the pack and slipped two fingers inside of his pants pocket, withdrawing a silver lighter. He remained relaxed against the brick wall as he lit another, casually blowing smoke rings as if he had all the time in the world, although now that she thought about it, he probably did.

"I'm trying to quit, or at a least cut back," Summer remarked, pointing to his cigarette. She tried her best to appear laissez-faire and not tip him off that she knew his secret. Releasing the spent butt from her hand, she ground it out with the toe of her shoe. The vampire remained silent, raising his cigarette to his lips and inhaling deeply.

"I'm down to less than half a pack a day now," she offered. The vampire responded by puffing out a series of tight smoke rings that orbited skyward, before dissipating into the darkness. "You know you really shouldn't chain smoke. It's very bad for your health," she heard herself ramble. The stranger threw his head back and laughed. Summer glimpsed the points of his fangs glinting in the light of the full moon, a momentary reminder that this was no ordinary man. She wondered if the display was deliberate, or if he simply didn't care if she knew.

Even without seeing his fangs or the flame, she would have known. Over the years, she had learned to recognize a physical response whenever a vampire came in close proximity - twenty feet or less. As if they were a magnet and she was steel, her body would respond with a sense of being pulled towards them, and she felt this reaction now. Although she knew with certainty what he was, there wasn't yet any indication that he was aware she knew.

"You are probably right." He tossed his cigarette to the pavement. "I suppose there are many things that are bad for our health, but it doesn't stop us from being attracted to them nevertheless."

With languid strides he crossed the alley, holding out his hand and saying, "Forgive me for not formally introducing myself. I am Lucien du Charmont."

So there it was - the caller and the vampire *were* one and the same. She reflexively offered her hand and, when she did, he raised it to his mouth; his touch not deathly cold as she had expected, but warm with life-blood.

He pressed his lips to her skin with such great reverence and refinement that Summer nearly expected him to genuflect before her.

In that moment, it was as if he wrapped her in the comfort of a warm blanket. She felt no fear, only the magnetic pull growing ever stronger, swelling until her ears rang as it pushed against her eardrums.

His lips lingered on her flesh for a long moment. As he began to release his hold on her hand, a wave of head-spinning vertigo swam through her with such a force that she clutched tightly onto his fingers to steady her legs, lest she crumple to the ground. His hand slipped to the small of her back, supporting her while she regained her balance, strength radiating from his fingertips as if he might sweep her up effortlessly with a single hand.

"Are you alright?" he asked. "Perhaps you should sit down for a minute."

As suddenly as it had come, the vertigo vanished. In its wake, a searing rush of embarrassment crept up her neck and burned her cheeks.

"No, no, I think I'm okay now." Summer dropped her head so he wouldn't see her go red in the face. "I promise that I don't usually have fainting spells every time someone introduces themselves."

"Ah, well then, should I be flattered or insulted?"

"Uh, probably neither," she replied, flustered. "It's just been a long, weird night. I'm pretty tired, I guess."

She was tired, true, but also confused and unnerved by the vampire Lucien du Charmont. He seemed in no hurry to confess his purpose, and Summer was impatient and curious by nature.

"Are you...did you call me tonight?" she asked, raising her gaze to finally meet the vampire face to face.

He was a good foot taller, and she had to tilt her chin upward to scan his face, which was fully visible now in the light that spilled through the doorway. He had the sort of male beauty which is so smooth and delicate it is nearly feminine. He was youthful, perhaps no more than twenty-one or two. His features quite defined; chiseled cheekbones, angular jaw line, aquiline nose and full, pouty lips punctuated by a small cleft in his chin. Locks of sandy-colored hair cascaded in long waves which framed his face, imparting him with a leonine appearance. She found his eyes to be most fascinating, as she could not discern with certainty the exact color of the mystifying orbs. They appeared to frequently change - always subtly altering so you could never really get a good look at them.

She mentally awarded him a full five out of five "Glory holes with a Reach-Around" - the highest score of hotness she'd ever bestowed upon a man.

The vampire placed his hand over his heart. "I confess, I called you," he said as if he were a wayward boy coming clean about some shameful act.

"It's not my fault, really," he continued, fixing his eyes on Summer with an intensity that caused her to squirm.

"Your dazzling voice is the culprit. One word and I was a fan."

It wasn't the first time she had heard similar remarks, her voice being deep, sultry and a tad breathy... the best sort of female voice for radio...

or phone sex. Summer raised an eyebrow knowingly and chuckled.

"Oh, you've heard this before," he said, dejectedly. "I know that it sounds clichéd," he went on. "but it speaks to me."

She didn't see it happen, but in less than an instant the space between them had grown smaller. He was so near that she could see the buttons of his shirt rise and fall with his breathing.

"It arouses my passions," he whispered, "and my passions are so rarely aroused these days."

She felt the stroke of his fingers on her cheek, but when she reached to brush his touch from her face, she saw that both of his hands were shoved inside of his pockets. A wicked smile crossed his face.

Tiny shivers tiptoed across her shoulders. He was fucking with her mind again - putting her off guard with his discomforting tricks. She should be pissed off, but he was so unapologetically bold, and she liked it more than a little bit. In fact, it was turning her on, and erotic imaginings flashed through her mind...the weight of his body crushing hers, fingers and tongues roaming one another's landscape, the feel of his...

"Summer, I hope my honesty hasn't made you uncomfortable." The vampire peered deeply into her eyes, and then dropped his gaze, moving backward a single pace; the distance just enough to break the mounting sexual tension and put her back to rights.

Straightening her backbone, she mustered what was left of her courage. "Frankly, it does. It makes me a little uncomfortable." Vampire or no vampire, she wasn't someone he could play with. "And if we are being honest here, certain parts of your call made me uncomfortable too." Summer squared her shoulders. "I have never met you before, and it seems you know a little too much about me."

She tried to speak politely - didn't want to piss him off - but despite of his head-turning allure, she was tiring of this cat and mouse game.

The vampire crossed his arms over his chest, cocking his head to the side. "What's the expression?" He raised his eyes in thought. "Oh yes. Tit for tat!" he exclaimed, snapping his finger and pointing at her. "It seems that you know a great deal about me as well. A great deal that I am not terribly comfortable with either."

Summer swallowed, her throat feeling drier than mummy pussy, and she cursed herself for opening her big, stupid mouth on the air tonight. So much for trying to hide being a Perceiver; the cat was out of the bag. Perhaps this was his mission; he was an envoy from the undead community. A warning, a threat or two, and he would be on his way. If being a Perceiver put her in danger she couldn't be sure, but her instincts detected no immediate threat from the vampire Lucien du Charmont.

She stared him squarely in the face. "I guess what we have here is a Mexican standoff."

The vampire knitted his brow in confusion. "I don't think I understand this Mexico standoff reference."

Summer laughed and slapped her hand on his shoulder. "It's a Mexi*can* standoff, and it means that we are in a situation where no one can win…like two people who each have a gun pointed at the other's head." The vampire seized Summer's hand from his shoulder, shocking her from her laughter. She tried to pull away, but he held a beggar's grip on her arm. Recalculating her position in the situation, she wondered if she'd been too hasty with her trust, as a ribbon of perspiration trailed the length of her spine.

"Are you frightened of me?" he asked.

Her heart thumped against her ribcage as his grip constricted the blood flow, numbing her fingers. "Should I be?" she breathed.

"That depends." He brought her wrist near his mouth. Summer wanted to cry out, but only a small croak came from her throat. "On whether I'm here to fuck you or feed on you."

The vampire loosened his grip, and turned her hand to his mouth, placing a kiss in the center of her palm, and she found her entire body once again swooning to his touch. A sigh, wistful as an April breeze, sang from her lips, as she said dreamily, "I didn't know those two options were mutually exclusive."

The vampire briefly patted the back of her hand before releasing it from custody. "They aren't; however, I am a man of chivalry." Placing his right hand over his heart, he dipped his head in deference. "I never feed on what I fuck." "Well then, my guess is that I have nothing to fear," she bantered, tossing her hair and looking him in the eye.

His gaze roamed undaunted over her face and body, making her want to cover her breasts with her arms, as if she were naked.

"You are very beautiful, but you do not have the slightest idea of it." A flush of heat inched up Summer's neck. "Excuse me, Mr. du Charmont, but are you trying to seduce me?" "Yes, Mademoiselle, I am. Is it working?" Oh, it was working alright. Most men bought her a drink or two - if she was lucky - then tried to dry hump her on the dance floor and expected her to swoon at their feet. But this guy, he was old school - flowery phrases and smoldering gazes - which delighted and bewitched her. He knew how to make her feel special and admired, like something precious.

"Would you walk awhile with a lonely vampire and allow me the opportunity to know you better?" he asked.

Her heart yearned to go with him. Her head, on the other hand, needed some convincing. To be so close to one of these creatures; not only close, but also *seduced* by one of them, was like a waking dream. Was she perhaps so enraptured as to be mortally foolish? She felt like Alice, perched on the edge of the rabbit hole, wavering on whether to take the plunge into the dark, mysterious unknown, and she was almost there… almost there…almost there…

"I can't. I have a show." Summer protested, mentally pulling her foot from the hole at the last minute. Her work responsibilities were her last line of defense against his irresistible persuasion.

"Melody can handle the callers," Lucien said hypnotically, hooking her arm in his. "She's obviously into pain."

"No, I can't…really…" she pulled back toward the building, making one final weak protest.

"I promise you will be safe," he reassured, his ever-changing eyes entreating her more urgently.

"Yeah, yeah, yeah…famous last words." The vampire's eyes scanned her from head to toe like some unearthly MRI machine,

"Frankly, for feeding purposes, you are not at all my type," he said.

Not his type? Should she be relieved or insulted? She supposed that if his plan was to attack her, he wouldn't waste time with all of this coaxing. He could have pounced, fed, and tomorrow she'd be merely another missing person.

"Okay, you win," she acquiesced. "But not too long or too far; I'm on the clock, you know."

"As am I," he said, indicating the moon which bowed towards the horizon.

Summer viewed the sinking orb, and her heart sank a bit too, as she realized that her time with the vampire was ticking away.

She allowed herself to be led, peering over her shoulder with a final fleeting look, as the exit door slowly swung closed and Alice plummeted into Wonderland.

***

As Summer strolled down the narrow street on the arm of Lucien du Charmont, the clip-clop of their footsteps echoed through the cement canyon. Inexplicably, she wasn't the least bit frightened. She was fascinated.

Despite his preternaturally pale flesh, his touch was warm. With her peripheral vision, she tried to inconspicuously scrutinize him.

"Trying to determine how I differ from mortal men?"

Summer rapidly averted her gaze, embarrassed that he'd caught her looking.

"Here, let's step under this streetlamp," he continued, guiding her into the illumination. "Look at me, Summer, go on. Here, take my hand and examine it. Is it the hand of a man or a monster?"

She held his hand in hers. His long tapered fingers tickled the sensitive flesh on the underside of her wrist. The polished glass appearance of his fingernails glinted in the lunar light. Blue veins criss-crossed his hand, a blood-filled road map of watery streams coursing beneath his skin. A gold signet ring impressed with a fleur de lis adorned his index finger.

There was something so overtly sexual about him. She'd heard the term "animal magnetism" but never encountered it until now. He threw off this vibe which made her want to knock his gorgeous ass down on the pavement and fuck him six ways to Sunday.

"Mr. du Charmont," she challenged, "what exactly do you want from me?"

The vampire brushed the back of his fingers along her neck, and it was as if a thousand spiders crawled down her spine.

Lucien gazed into her icy-blue eyes and wondered how he might possibly explain to her his desperate craving for companionship. Loneliness stalked him like a persistent panhandler, and too long he'd denied himself the warmth and comfort of mortals. He yearned to recall the willing touch of a human - to sense something other than fear seeping from their skin - to feel like a man again. He had once been mortal, and remembered all too well the terror that his kind struck into the hearts of the living.

In this woman he recognized a kindred spirit. She, too, dwelt in the seclusion of the darkened hours, reaching out to those she could never truly know. She fed on her callers' miserable lives, as he might feed on their miserable blood, both solitary creatures with insatiable appetites to comprehend the void which existed in their lives.

When Summer had revealed that she was a Perceiver, he had known that he could wait no longer. He had to meet her.

Lucien was certain she would recognize him for what he was - that her curiosity would be piqued long enough for him to steal a few precious moments with her -sufficient time to coax her out of fear and into the light of knowledge.

"Please call me Lucien," he implored, cradling her hand in his; her pulse beating determinedly beneath the supple flesh.

"Night after night I listen to people revealing their secrets to you," he sighed. "I also need to unburden my soul, and I need you to be my confessor of sorts because," he continued. "too long, I have walked in the shadows, keeping my secrets, both wonderful and terrible. I want to know you and for you to know me." The subtle aroma of her female musk wafted into his nostrils, distracting him, his ultra-keen senses exposing what she concealed between her thighs. His cock stirred, nagging for release from the snug confines of his jeans. "You want to get to know me?" she asked, arching her eyebrow in suspicion.

Lucien placed his palms flat against the brick wall on either side of her shoulders. "Intimately," he whispered. "I want to know what you think, what you feel, and how you taste when I kiss you. I want to learn what you like and what you don't, what makes you laugh and what makes you weep." He heard the beating of her heart quicken to a fevered pace. It fluttered against the silk of her white blouse as she swallowed hard, her trachea rising against the gulp.

"Why me?" her husky voice was barely audible.

If she hadn't worn heels, he would have towered over her petite frame, but as he stood with his body inches from hers, his chest was even with the level of her eyes. He smelled her hair, and it was like crisp green apples. Lucien recalled the scent but not the taste.

He sighed deeply. "I chose you because you are a collector of stories."

She shifted her stance, her knee lightly brushing against his thigh as she propped her foot on the wall behind her. "I chose you because I sensed that you would not fear me and because I don't have to pretend I am something I am not with you."

She was very quiet and attentive, her eyes focused on the movement of his lips.

Lucien cupped her chin, tilting her eyes towards his. "You already see what I am. I want you to see *who* I am."

See me, he willed. *Perceive beyond your fascination, and witness what lies at the heart of me.*

A shallow pool of tears welled in her eyes, a salty drop running down her cheek. He caught it with the tip of his finger, his long-dead heart leaping with gratitude for that single tiny tear.

"I want to take you into my world and prove to you and to myself that I am more than my thirst, more than the murderer the world believes me to be."

She knitted her brow, nodding her head in understanding. Lucien felt that his secrets would be safe with her. He longed for the absolution of the confessional, and she would be his confessor.

"I seek redemption for the things that I have done and those that I have failed to do."

He detected no trace of judgment in her eyes. Her face bore only lovely compassion.

"Oh, Mr. du Charm..." She stumbled on the words as if she weren't certain if she should speak his name.

"You are beautiful, and daring, and exciting to me." He pressed his body nearer to hers, and it emboldened him when she did not protest or recoil.

"You are also solitary and thoughtful...and lonely. You see what others do not, and I hope that you may see something in me that I cannot."

The warmth of her eyes reminded him of the warmth of the sun which had not touched his face since that fateful day so long ago. He recalled the bright colors of a long-forgotten garden of his youth, nestled in a green hillside above a wide, wandering stream. Summer - it was more than her name - it was her definition. With her, he felt as if he might once again experience that most glorious of seasons, where he basked in a sun-dappled meadow, the hum of bees buzzing from blossom to blossom, songbirds calling to their mates from distant branches... the entire world stirring with warmth and life.

Lucien felt a desire that he had not known for many lifetimes. He wanted to roll in verdant groves with this woman, to feel the cool dewiness of grass on his naked skin, to nestle in the gentleness of her form, inhaling her scent and savoring her flavors. Over the centuries, he had not denied himself female comforts, but it had always been only a necessary thing - lustful encounters serving to satisfy physical needs. This felt different. He wasn't compelled to dive headlong into possessing her. He knew that, by consuming her blood, all of her secrets would be revealed, but he didn't want them that way. He yearned to coax them from her slowly and deliberately - to touch that place where the human heart lies and to prove to himself that, somewhere, his heart still beat with a similar cadence.

Summer tried to wrap her mind around the emotions that she was feeling. This man was a monster - a hunter of humans. Yet she felt profound compassion and attraction. Was it the work of his unholy magic or something real?

Vampires had always seemed like powerful, commanding beings - wild things bereft of conscience and morals. Summer never imagined that beneath their fierce façade might lay weakness and self-doubt. Perhaps they were not so far removed from humans after all.

She burned with curiosity to know more about Lucien du Charmont. He was a savage thing, but not without emotion, and perhaps his condition caused him to feel emotions even more keenly than mortals.

There was desperation in his voice, a desperation that cried for redemption from his deeds; but she was no one special, and certainly not anyone's savior.

Summer backed against the bricks, the delicate fabric of her blouse snagging on the rough mortar that seeped from the cracks in the wall.

"Lucien," she began, "I think you have the wrong girl. I'm not what you hear on the radio. That's a personality, a shtick." Even as Summer spoke the words, she hoped that she was wrong.

"And I am not what you have read in books or seen in movies." Lucien entreated, stepping so near to her that she glimpsed the points of his fangs. She was torn between recoiling and longing to see them in full.

His hands gripped her arms, refocusing her attention to his imploring eyes.

"All I am asking is that you give me a chance to show you the truth behind the fables, and perhaps, along the way, I can find a way to find peace with what I have become."

His sturdy shoulders sank with the guilty weight of his words. Summer observed his eyes change from green to grey, then violet. A strong look of intent crossed his face.

Her sexual attraction to him was undeniable. It oozed from every pore of her body. But her fascination with the vampire was more than physical. She felt a compelling emotional attraction, and she sensed that she was, by some means, inextricably intertwined with him; that if she turned him away, her life would be somehow less.

At this moment, he seemed to her entirely human, with all of the needs, wants, desires and frailties of a mortal man. Her paradigms shifted, and everything she thought she had known about vampires seemed trite and superficial. Her stereotypical assumptions falling away one by one, she burned with shame at her ignorance.

"Alright," she said, nodding her head in agreement. "You have your chance. I'll agree to be your confidante, but at the first whiff of something funny, I'm done with it. You got that?"

One corner of the vampire's mouth turned up in a half-smile. "I understand, and, in return, I give you my promise that you will be under my protection."

Wait a second; he hadn't said anything about this being dangerous enough to need protection. As if reading her thoughts, Lucien held a finger to her lips.

"Shhh…no worries. Shall we seal the agreement in the traditional French way - with a kiss?" he asked.

Before she could dissent, he planted a kiss on her right cheek. When he moved his head to kiss the left side of her face, she turned her mouth in the direction of his. She didn't know what made her do it; it just happened.

His lips were lush, full of promised pleasure. Her tongue slipped into his open mouth, and she guided the tip of her probing tongue along the edge of his teeth searching for the fabled fangs, wanting to examine them with her tongue. Locating one of the pointed incisors, she licked it, shallowly slicing her tongue on a razor-edged point. A drop of blood flowed from her tongue and, in the dark filth of the alleyway, she tasted the metallic flavor of her own hemoglobin as it bled into his mouth. In the recesses of her mind, Summer knew that she had tasted sin. Clutching his belt buckle, she pulled him tightly against her body.

Lucien held her face in his hands, his eager mouth engulfing hers.

She had questioned whether vampires possessed working equipment.

The answer to that question now pressed hotly against her thigh. The vampire Lucien du Charmont was undeniably equipped with a soldier of love and it was mustering for action.

The pink buds of her breasts swelled and pushed against the lacy fabric of her bra, and she pressed her body forcefully to his, devouring his mouth, while her fingers caressed his muscled back. The marble-like quality of his flesh contrasted sharply to the softness of hers. His body felt powerful, lean and taut like a cheetah, all elongated muscle and sinew, without an ounce of excess fat to slow its swiftness.

His mouth sought the sensitive flesh of her neck and as his lips touched her there, she became awash with the bliss of sweet surrender. Sighing, she bowed her neck, willingly exposing the tender veins which pulsed entreatingly beneath the surface. His breath tiptoed across her skin like little cat paws; the whole of her body trembling as he sucked her flesh into his mouth. There was no pain, no point of fangs, only unbearable ecstasy rushing through her limbs and sweeping through her core as the vampire caressed her neck with his fervent kiss.

She clung forcefully to him, feeling as if the deliciousness of it all would cause her to dissolve in his embrace until there was nothing left of her but a small wisp of smoke; as if she were melting in a fire which consumed but did not burn.

The startling sound of metal clattering to the pavement awakened Summer from her rapturous trance. She withdrew from Lucien, searching the darkness for the source of the clamor, but not locating it. As profoundly as she had been swept into the hurricane of his embrace, she now foundered, disoriented in the stillness of his wake.

The vampire's eyes scanned the night sky for signs of change. A gradual luminosity crept into the stratosphere; an arc of glowing indigo perched on the horizon. He didn't want to leave, but he must. They spoke the words at the same time. "I have to go."

In the damp alley, under the glare of a streetlamp, Lucien held Summer in his arms one last time, inhaling the fresh scent of her hair, committing it to memory.

With a heart full of longing, he released her, watching protectively as she scurried back to the familiar security of the mortal world.

Behind a high window in the KJZM building, he spied a shadow moving in the darkness.

Down for the Count

"Summer, where in the hell have you been?" Melody demanded, as she bolted out of the sound booth with wide eyes and flailing arms. "I was getting ready to call the cops!"

As Melody's gaze swept her from head to foot, Summer became acutely aware of her disheveled appearance.

"What the fuck happened to you, Summer? Are you alright?"

Melody's questioning was at once unnerving and irritating. Her interrogation made Summer feel like a teenager who had violated curfew.

"It's nothing, Melody. I tripped down the stairs a little, that's all," she lied, straightening her skirt. Her encounter with Lucien was personal, private and not something she was willing to share just yet. She wanted only for the night to be over, so that she could bask in the memory while it was still fresh in her mind.

"Wait; is that a hickey on your neck? Let me see?" Melody's eyes widened as she moved towards her to obtain a closer look.

"Where? No, of course not," her hand instinctively obscuring the spot where Lucien had placed his mouth. "I haven't had a hickey since high school; don't be ridiculous."

Melody turned her attention to the control board muttering, "It looks like a hickey to me." Her fingers traced the tender welt where the vampire's mouth had been; the memory of his kiss still lingered on her skin. She released her hair from the number two pencil which held it in place, fanning it to shelter her bruised neck.

She had to wrap things up at the studio and get out before Melody renewed the Spanish Inquisition.

Headphones in place, Summer rolled her chair to the microphone.

"You're listening to KJZM late night talk radio, and this is Summer Solstice, wishing all of my listeners a wonderful weekend. I'll be back with you on Monday at one o'clock in the a.m. Next up, to get you moving through your day is KJZM's own wacky morning team: Wildman and Woofer."

**

Summer looked up at the old licorice factory which had stood sentinel over the city of St. Louis since 1874. It had been vacant and decaying for over three decades; its sprawling painted sign fading against the red brick. But now the imposing structure was rehabbed and revitalized, providing panoramic views of the waterfront and the narrow cobblestone streets of Laclede's Landing. The fortunate few who resided in its apartments enjoyed the building's close proximity to the pulse points of the city. She was one of those fortunate few, snagging a top floor loft at a bargain price before renovations had even begun.

Entering the elevator, she relished the hushed silence of the building, adequately soundproofed against the roar and hum of the city streets; a necessity for someone on the night shift. The security system was state of the art too, providing a single woman with a needed sense of protection in this oftentimes dodgy metropolis.

Arriving at her loft, she stepped from the private elevator that led into her apartment, pulling the iron gate over the door and locking it securely. Early morning sunlight streamed through the oversized windows. Summer kicked off her shoes, spooned cereal into a bowl, and stood by the panoramic window to watch the boats chug lazily down the Mississippi River. Her eyes followed The Becky Thatcher, an old paddle wheeler cruising tourists along the muddy waters, as she recalled her encounter with the vampire Lucien du Charmont.

True, it was unconventional to say the least, but she was a grown-ass woman of thirty who had known her share of unconventional lovers along the way. She had even "gone down to girly town" once or twice in college. Live and let live. If someone is attracted to someone, she rationalized, why not do what comes naturally?

If Lucien were human, he would be exactly the physical type she would be attracted to…except for the age thing. If he were human, she would probably look but not touch. Boyish young men brought out the whole "Coo-coo-ca-choo Mrs. Robinson" vibe in her. But he wasn't human. He was a vampire…a sexy, enthralling, dangerous vampire. In the light of day, she wondered if she was playing with fire, but, like a pyromaniac, she was fascinated by the flame.

Her absorption with vampires had been brewing since the day her eyes first perceived the tell-tale blue glow, which she later learned was their soul flame, hovering just above their heads.

She made a habit of spying on them as they moved amongst the throngs of revelers in Laclede's Landing, the city's vibrant entertainment district, whose narrow streets and secluded alleyways provided a fertile hunting ground. Like a naturalist tracking an elusive species, she watched them from afar, always keeping a careful distance.

Typically, like Lucien, they tried to blend in with society. They dressed like anyone else, some had fine tastes and some were seriously fashion-challenged. They came in all shapes and sizes, but as a rule, they were extraordinarily beautiful. Perhaps many were chosen for their loveliness alone.

Lucien was an exceptional example. He was one of the beautiful boys - frozen in time while the tender bloom of youth still blessed his face.

She wondered why she had never seen him before. Perhaps he hunted a different area, or could conceal himself at will. The more she discovered about these creatures, the less she found she knew.

Sometimes, as she strolled along the congested brick streets, she felt their eyes picking her out of the crowd. She was certain the older, more experienced ones recognized her as a Perceiver - an identity that could easily land her in serious trouble. Still she chose to live in the midst of them, ever inquisitive and watchful of their habits. Never had she imagined that one might be observing her with the same curiosity and interest.

The moment under the streetlight with Lucien was the culmination of her lifelong fascination with these elusive creatures. She had longed for such a moment, and now, having had the experience, she was not fearful or filled with regret. She was elated.

Later that morning, after showering and changing into a satin chemise for sleeping, she lay awake in bed trying to fix the details of the momentous event into her memory for safekeeping.

***

Summer awakened in the darkness. Red LED lights on her bedside clock announced the time as nine-o-seven. Saturday night and she had no plans. She wondered what Melody was doing and thought about inviting her out for a drink. Maybe not. Melody was certain to pummel her with questions about her absence the night before last. She wasn't yet prepared to share her experience with anyone. Even though Lucien hadn't asked her to keep their meeting a secret, she sensed that somehow she would be breaking a trust if she didn't.

Who was she kidding? There was only one person that she wanted to see tonight. She yearned for his company like an addict for a drug, wondering when she would get her next fix.

Summer shifted restlessly in her bed. Maybe she would go hang around the Landing. It was a long shot, but she might run into Lucien there.

Throwing the covers back, she turned on the radio. The Eagles' *Green Eyed Lady* crooned from the speakers. Feeling buoyed by the prospect of another encounter with the vampire Lucien du Charmont, she danced and swayed to the tune. Dipping and spinning into the living room, she flipped on the light switch and was stupefied to see Lucien standing at her window, looking out at the city below. He turned from the window more rapidly than her eyes could perceive.

One moment he was looking out the window and the next, he was facing her, but she could not see the mercurial shift of his body.

"Mon dieu," he said, placing his hand over his heart, "you startled me!"

Her heart leap-frogged into her throat, as her eyes darted to the still bolted locks on the gate. How had he breached them without setting off the alarm?

"Well, we're even, then. You scared the shit out of me!" As much as she was relieved to know that her intruder wasn't some unknown assailant in a ski mask, it didn't relieve the hollow, unsettling feeling of violation inside of her.

"You can't just pop in on people like this," she chided, hands on hips. "It's just not right."

Lucien stared blankly at his shoes. "Forgive me. It's been a long while since I have had to consider the constraints of your world."

"Well, you seriously need to be domesticated!" Even though she scolded him, the initial shock of finding him in her apartment was wearing off. Her heart no longer pounded, and the itchy irritation at his intrusion slipped away like a petal on a swift stream.

He didn't reply, instead turning slowly to gaze out of the window.

The hand of remorse slapped her upside the head, sharply reprimanding her for the flip comment.

"Hey, I'm sorry," she offered. "I really didn't mean that." She inched closer to him, hoping he would turn to look at her. "Sometimes smartass stuff just comes out of my mouth. It's an occupational hazard."

Finally, he turned to her again, a Cheshire cat grin spanning his face. "Would you like to tame me? See me content to lap little saucers of milk from your cupboard?"

His remarks chastised her. He was a wild thing. His beauty and attraction lay in his feral nature. She would no more enjoy seeing him tamed than she did seeing animals in cages.

"No," she conceded with a wave of her hand. "No, I don't want to tame you."

"Nor I you, my little fierce one," he replied with a wink.

Summer plopped down on the couch, tucking her too-revealing chemise around her bare thighs.

"So, what *are* you doing here?" she queried.

"I've come to take you on a proper date."

"A date?"

"Yes, mon chérie, a date. You are familiar with the term?"

She raised a skeptical eyebrow.

Lucien paced in front of her, like a college professor in a lecture hall. "You dress in something fetching. I take you out on the town, ply you with drinks, we laugh and flirt shamelessly with one another…" he pivoted sharply on his toes, facing her straight on, "…then you coyly invite me into your apartment to see your collection of little porcelain poodles with the funny spaghetti hair…" He smiled a cunning smile. "… But what you really want to know is if I would like to come inside for a little scotch and sofa."

How delightful, innuendo and blue humor, her favorite kind! She could see they were going to get along just fine.

With a grand flourish, he proffered his hand in invitation. "Would you care to accompany me on a date, Mademoiselle?"

Oh hell, yes she would, she thought, as her gaze swept from his lean, long legs to his tousled wavy hair. As far as she was concerned, he could keep his drinks and dancing and cut straight to the scotch and sofa part. Her knees grew weak at the thought of it.

Standing at the window with the starlit sky as a backdrop, he looked good enough to eat. Perhaps he was thinking the same thing about her.

She sauntered to him as seductively as a cat on the prowl. Her fingers played with the buttons on his plum-toned shirt, "I would very much enjoy going on a date with you. But you are wrong about one thing."

He raised an eyebrow inquisitively.

"I won't be asking you in to view my collection of porcelain poodles."

"Non?" he replied in French.

Summer shook her head regretfully, turning the corners of her mouth into a frown. "No, I'm sorry I won't," she said, secretly relishing the look of disappointment on his face. Rising on tiptoe, she whispered in his ear. "I'll ask if you would like to see my collection of Verve Jazz recordings."

Lucien's arms wrapped around her waist, and he pulled her to him with a moan. She melted into him, imagining their clothing falling away and the feel of his bare flesh against hers.

"I will have to warn you," he purred, "the sound of a Jazz saxophone gives me a tremendous erection."

The intoxicating thought of his vampiric prick sent her head to spinning. She entwined her fingers in his caramel-hued hair, allowing the glossy strands to slowly slip through her fingertips. He was forbidden fruit and how she longed for a taste.

Tilting her mouth towards his, she petitioned for a kiss, but Lucien gently broke the embrace.

"Dress quickly, chérie," he advised, "there is much that I want to share with you. The night is impatient."

***

Summer wore her conceit like a suit of fine armor as she strolled on the arm of the handsome vampire.

She adored the way she looked, her deep-plunge black halter dress hugging her curves to perfection, with her navel piercing glinting through the sheer mesh insert that encircled her waist. The flirty skirting swayed seductively around her thighs as her patent pumps glided along the sidewalk. Lucien's already arresting appearance presented the epitome of chic. His plum shirt accented his long latte locks, and the fit of his charcoal grey wool trousers showed off an ass so firm you could bounce a quarter off of it. As they squeezed their way through the crowded riverfront streets, she clung tightly to Lucien's arm, for fear she might float away from the sheer delight of it all.

Time and the crush of people seemed to fade into the distance as they wound through a maze of streets and alleyways. She contentedly followed Lucien's lead, not caring where they were going.

He stopped before a small doorway. In all of her forays into the night life of the Landing, Summer had never noticed this spot.

A dimly lit sign announced the entrance to *Down for the Count.*

"A sports bar?" she laughed. "Are you taking me to a sports bar?" "Not exactly," he said, holding the door open for her. The pulsing rhythms of techno music assaulted her ears. Swirling colors of light swept in wide arcs over the patrons inside.

"Well, Waddaya know! Lucien, where you been hiding?" barked a voice with an accent Summer recognized as distinctly New Jersey. "And who's da doll wid you? I don't think I've had da pleasure of her acquaintance." The beefy vampire, smartly attired in full-on Dracula garb, leered at her, boldly undressing her with his eyes.

"Summer this is Gino—Gino, Summer."

Gino kissed her hand. Lucien's arm tightened around her waist reassuringly.

"Pleased to make your acquaintance," Gino said, adjusting his cummerbund.

"Seven dollar cover tonight," Gino informed. "Each."

Lucien handed the money to the acne-scarred man. "Where would youse like to sit? I have a nice private corner table in da back."

"Thanks for the offer there, Vlad," he quipped, "but tonight, nobody puts Baby in the corner. A center table please, we want to be in the action."

Summer found Lucien's pop culture assimilation amusing. She'd never really thought about vampire evolution. She had held the notion that they would be perpetually stuck in the era which had spawned them. She realized now what a ludicrous belief that had been. Mortals did not remain static, so why should vampires?

Gino led them to a small, round table, circled halfway by a high-backed, tufted banquette. The caped bouncer pulled out the table with a flourish, its metal legs scraping against the concrete floor. He motioned for Summer to be seated. As she lowered herself onto the white leather, Gino graciously held her hand to steady her descent. She wasn't certain if she was in a scene from Dracula or the Godfather. Lucien slid onto the bench from the opposite side.

"Ted's gonna be your server tonight. Have a nice time, youse two." Gino handed them each a tall menu, and waddled back to his post near the doorway.

"Ted? Don't tell me that there is a vampire named Ted?" Summer laughed. "Well, of course. Not all vampires have romantic and mysterious names. Some of us have to be named Ted and Joe and even Marcia. However, many change their names because they want to sound more fearsome, or they want to give the illusion that they are much older than they actually are."

She shifted nervously in her seat. She might as well face it. She was a tourist in a foreign land, and obviously she hadn't the slightest notion how to speak the language. She made a mental note to try to not put her foot in her mouth for the rest of the night.

"I suppose," Lucien continued, placing his index finger to his cheek thoughtfully, "they feel that they will be more respected. Just like your name is not really Summer Solstice." He raised his brow knowingly, touching the tip of her nose with his finger. "It is Summer Stone. It's the same principle with us."

How fascinating. Summer had learned more about vampires in five minutes with Lucien than she had in her entire life. She hungered to ingest every detail of this mysterious night.

"What about you, Lucien du Charmont? Is that your real name?" "Mmmm, it is." he replied, inching closer to her until his arm wrapped round her shoulder, and they sat face to face; shoulders connecting, thighs connecting, eyes connecting.

"Good, because I like it," she said. "It's fancy."

Summer placed her hand on Lucien's knee. She scarcely dared to think of him as a lover. The idea was appealing and appalling at the same time. Perhaps vampires made love in strange ways that she couldn't even imagine. Then again, perhaps they made love in wondrous ways that she couldn't yet dream!

"Would you like me to tell you a few things about myself or would that bore you?" he asked.

"Somehow I get the feeling that what you have to say is going to be anything but boring." Summer pulled a cigarette from her case, rooting in her purse for her silver lighter.

"Allow me," a voice emerged from behind an orange glow. She looked up to see a vampire offering her a light. She leaned into the flame; slowly dragging on her cigarette.

"I'm Ted," he informed. "I'll be your server tonight."

He was extremely thin and lanky, with an elongated face that reminded Summer of Stan Laurel. He wore black tuxedo pants, a cummerbund and a stiff white shirt that sported illuminated liquor advertisement buttons. One in particular caught her attention. It was a glittering green fairy, blinking to life in one place and then in another. It gave the illusion that she was flitting from one spot to the next on Ted's shoulder.

"Are you ready to order, or do you need a few minutes?" he asked.

"Brandy, please for me, and the lady will have..."

"I'll have a Cutty Sark on the rocks, double," said Summer, scanning the menu, "and how is the Nosferatuna melt?"

Ted screwed up his face and shook his head from side to side.

"Oh, that bad, huh? I think I will just wait awhile to eat." She closed the menu, handing it to Ted.

"I'm down with that," replied Ted. "I'll be back with your drinks in two shakes of a martini."

Summer surveyed the room. Vampires and mortals alike drank and danced, some mingling together, and some gathering in tightly packed cliques of separation. She noticed ironically, that other than the staff, the vampires were dressed quite normally, while the mortals were often dressed as vampires, as if they wanted to be that which they were not.

Fingers crept along her inner thigh, brushing the skin that was exposed just above her stocking.

"Are you enjoying yourself, Mon petit voyeur?" "Busted," she admitted, smiling guiltily at Lucien. Summer couldn't help her fascination with every aspect of this odd place. In her curiosity, she realized that she had been totally neglecting her escort.

"I'm sorry," she apologized, squeezing his knee. "I feel like a kid at Disneyland."

She turned to him to explain. "It's just so weird, because I thought I knew more than the average person about vampires." She placed her hand on Lucien's cheek, stroking it lovingly with her fingertips. "I realize now that I've always been on the outside with my nose pressed up against the glass, looking in, but never really being a part of it. Now I find I've dropped into their world, and I know nothing at all."

"Well, then, before I strain your ears with the sad story of my life, what would you like to know about the lives of the vampires?"

Summer picked up Lucien's arm, placing it around her shoulder, and

snuggled into him. "Everything, Lucien - I want to know everything."
While his fingertips languidly stroked her bare shoulder, occasionally
brushing against her breast, he whispered stories of the vampires into
her ear.

"See that mature lady standing at the bar - the cougar dressed in
Chanel with the silver hair pulled tightly into a chignon? Her name
is Patrice, and vanity is her sin. The story goes, so fearful was she of
growing older, that she begged to be turned into a vampire before she
aged another day. Now she prowls the city looking for youthful lovers
to feed her ego." Lucien exaggerated a shudder.

"That group in the corner, the one where the mortals are paired with
vampires; those are vampires and their 'Donors'. Donors are the most
pathetic of all creatures. They offer themselves to a vampire as food,
but the relationship never lasts. As all servants are wont to do, Donors
eventually desire to become like the master. Unfortunately, by that time,
their minds are too far gone, and they would make a dangerous and
cruel vampire. Rarely does a master turn a Donor." Summer surveyed
the congregation of Donors and Masters. The Donors gazed at their
vampire Masters sycophantically, while the vampires drank lustily from
their offered wrists and necks. For the first time since entering this den
of blood-thieves, Summer felt a cold chill in her bones.

"What happens to them?" Summer asked.

"You don't want to know." Lucien shook his head and waved his hand
as if to dismiss the offending answer. "If the master is kind, he finishes
them off. If he is selfish and uncaring, he abandons them to the streets."

Summer swallowed hard, her eyes roaming the group of Donors,
wondering what would become of each one. Who were these pitiful
people, and how did they arrive at this place in their lives? She wondered.

Lucien heaved a heavy sigh. "Sadly, there are legions of these
wretched shells walking the world, their minds so damaged and
twisted that they become serial killers, sexual deviants, and oftentimes
politicians." *Legions? Did he say legions?* The implications were staggering.

Summer was woozy at the possibility of so much sickness released
into the world.

"Mon chérie," Lucien warned. "Make note of the faces of the Donors
that you see here, because you cannot tell them from other humans."

Summer scanned the blank faces of the Donors. He was right. There
was nothing at all that distinguished them.

"These are very dangerous beings," he warned. "They seek to possess the power and control that has been exerted on them by their Masters, and they find many ways to feed their craving. Most of the horror unleashed on mankind is at the hands of abandoned Donors."

The information was a terror and a revelation at the same time. Summer pressed a little closer to Lucien as she turned the possibilities over in her mind. How many times had she watched a true crime show on TV and wondered aloud, "What kind of sick bastard could do something like that?" Now she knew.

Her thoughts were interrupted as Ted placed their drinks on the table. Lucien indicated that they did not need anything else for the moment. She took a long gulp of the amber liquid, trying to wash away the bitter taste in her mouth. She called to mind some of the infamous fiends of the world...Hitler, Dahmer, Manson, Gacy...could they have been Donors?

Lucien tapped her rapidly on the leg, pointing to a corner of the room. "See the group of vamps hustling unsuspecting suckers at billiards - their names are Marcus, Gaston, Dodger and Nitro. They call themselves the Vicious Ones, and I recommend steering clear of them."

Summer turned her attention to the gang of four. They were young, modern-day vampires, dressed in black leather jackets with an odd embroidered symbol on the back.

One of them knocked over a drink onto the green felt of the pool table, and the others loudly berated him for his clumsiness. On the surface, they appeared no different from any other rowdy gang of miscreants that might be found hanging out in a club.

Lucien then pointed his chin to the bar area where a forlorn, middle-aged fellow slumped over the polished countertop.

"See the puffy-faced vampire sitting next to the barfly?" he continued. "That's Louie the Lush. He was a drunk when he was turned, and now he feeds only on alcoholics. He waits until his victim is besotted with booze, and then he tames two beasts with one bite." The stories of the vampires were many and varied. With deepening concern, Summer pondered what Lucien's story might be.

Whom did he choose to feed on? She didn't like the thought of him feeding at all. Did she even want to know? She wanted to see him as pure and guiltless, but the sickening reality was that it just couldn't be. Did he prey on helpless women? Little children? The very thought nauseated her, and she tried to push it from her mind. Surely, he wouldn't, but she had no way of knowing without directly asking him.

"You see," he continued. "Vampires tend to retain their mortal natures after they turn. If a vampire was merciful as a mortal, they will also be merciful as a vampire. If a mortal has a cruel nature, he will continue to do battle with those same cruel urges as a vampire."

It made perfect sense to Summer. People don't generally change who they truly are no matter the circumstances. A skunk doesn't become a rose and vice versa. She contemplated her interactions with Lucien, searching for clues to his nature.

Tonight he had been gentle and protective, but there had been moments in the alley where he seemed to enjoy frightening her. Had he been testing her, or did he hide a secret sadistic streak?

The question of his feeding habits hounded her with the doggedness of a bounty hunter. If she was going to be keeping company with this vampire, she needed to know, but she truly didn't want to know because, once she knew, she would have to decide if she could live with the answer.

"And you?" she broached. "What kind of vampire are you and who do you choose to feed on?"

The question hung heavily in the air. Summer had put it out there, testing the waters. The driving beat of the dance music pounded in her ears as she awaited the vampire's response.

Lucien withdrew his touch, placing both hands flat upon the table, his eyes clouded as he stared straight ahead. Summer chewed her lip, as the silence grew pregnant with anxiety.

If the question tormented him, she could not tell. His face was impenetrably sphinx-like. She wished now that she could take it back. Her hands began to tremble, and she clasped them tightly together.

Finally, with eyes cast downward he released a leaden sigh and confessed. "Only the lonely - I feed on only the lonely. Those beings that are so bereft of the will to go on, they not only welcome death's sweet release, they are grateful to me for doing what they do not have the courage to do for themselves."

He fixed his eyes on hers, the enigmatic orbs now as grey as thunderclouds.

"Those are my prey, Mon petit, and there are a good many of them in this city."

Summer understood exactly what he was saying. Only the lonely...

the familiar phrase reverberated in her head. She knew all too well about the loneliness that hung over this city like a damp blanket. She heard the tales of its effect five nights a week. There were occasions when certain despondent callers would simply cease phoning in. She wondered if their despair had caused them to take their own lives, or whether they had found some happiness and moved on. Perhaps it was neither. Perhaps it was Lucien.

Her heart went out to him, because the subject of his feeding seemed to torture him so. She looked at his face, wondering if it was the last thing his victims saw, and if its beauty comforted them at all.

Lucien remained silent, the muscles of his neck drawn tight. She took a deep breath, and looked into his ever-changing eyes. "It's okay, Lucien," she reassured. "I wanted to know, and you told me. I appreciate your honesty."

He had found the only way he could to cope with what he was, just as she accepted she could never be a vegetarian. She liked the taste of meat, and as long as it was packaged in neat little Styrofoam containers in the market, she didn't have to think about the animals that it came from or what they endured to give it.

In his case, there was no substitute for fresh human blood, no tidy little vampire supermarkets. He was doing the best he could with the hand he had been dealt. She would not judge him. He was already condemned.

Lucien inhaled sharply and clapped his hands together resolutely. "Enough of that talk," he said brightly. "You need another drink." He motioned to Ted. "Let me order for you this time. I want to take you on a journey back through time, and I know just the thing that will help you see more clearly."

Ted pulled a pen from behind his ear. "Another round?" he asked.

"Another brandy for me and bring the lady a Green Fairy." Ted cleared away the empty glasses. "One Picasso's Poison coming up!"

Flight of the Green Fairy

Summer gazed into the goblet at the hypnotic emerald liquid. The pungent scent of anise wafted from its glimmering depths. Her tongue slipped over her lips, moistening them in anticipation.

Absinthe. She had heard tales of this legendary liquor. Her heart quickened, as she grew impatient to taste its forbidden secrets.

Enraptured, she watched as Lucien's sculpted hands deftly performed the absinthe ritual which she had heard of, but never seen. With a small pair of silver tongs, Lucien plucked a sugar cube and dunked it quickly into the absinthe. He placed the sweet, sticky cube onto a slotted spoon which he balanced atop the goblet rim. Striking a match, he set fire to the sugar. As the absinthe burned off, the sugar dissolved into the emerald liquid forming undulating ribbons of milky opalescence in the thick elixir. When the flame burned low, Lucien stirred the brew with the slotted spoon until the last of the clear emerald liquid transformed into a creamy hue.

"Drink quickly," he instructed, "before it cools."

Summer put the goblet to her lips and drank deeply of the exotic concoction. It possessed a peculiarly bitter, yet pleasant taste. Its exquisite fragrance filled her head.

After a moment, her backbone relaxed as her mind grew clearer, a sense of bliss overwhelming every cell. The world assaulted her all at once. She breathed sounds and heard colors. Scents produced a sensation of lightness or of weight, roughness or smoothness, as if she were touching them with her fingers.

Summer felt a strong sense of empathy towards everyone and everything.

She leaned against the cool leather of the booth - Lucien's arm draped across the back - and she rested her head in the crook of his elbow. His hand cradled her shoulder, drawing her closer. She melted into him with the sense of their energies merging and mingling, as if two were becoming one.

Awash with a most delicious tranquility, her head lolled to one side, and her half-lidded eyes dropped drowsily downward. She passively noticed a single perfect bead of the enchanting elixir lay on the swell of her breast, oozing ever so slowly towards the crease of her cleavage. Turning toward Lucien, she saw his eyes fixed upon the errant droplet as well. Encircling her waist with his arm, his lips parted, and he retrieved the sweet syrup with the tip of his tongue.

A current of sexual energy ignited in her breast, crackling down the center of her torso, and detonating in her pussy like a Fourth of July sparkler.

The heat of her body rose, and she knew that it was more than the absinthe diffusing through her bloodstream. Despite the warm flush rising on her neck, she trembled as their eyes met.

With a feather-light touch, his fingers flitted over the mounds of her breasts, tracing the edges of the deep neckline of her dress. Her breath caught in her throat as she arched her back, her body eagerly greeting his touch.

Lights from the dance floor swirled through the darkness of the club and seemed to wrap them in garlands of living colors. Lucien drew her tightly to his body. She pressed her cheek to his. His skin felt cool and smooth. Her fingers entwining his hair, she yielded her neck to him and urged his mouth towards the vulnerable spot. With lingering kisses, his mouth caressed her neck, sucking at the flesh, but never piercing it.

Every moment was an eternity; every sensation brought such pleasure that she wasn't certain her body could contain it.

Lucien's fingers crept beneath her skirt and stroked the supple skin on her inner thigh; his cool touch against her warm flesh like fire and ice. She felt unmoored from herself, adrift from her body. The sights and sounds of the club faded into nothing more than background noise. She was aware only of his touch upon her thigh, and she longed for him to explore ever higher towards the moist heat between her legs.

Summer parted her thighs, urging him onward, but his hand stroked her thigh and nothing more. The scent of his desire, drenched in deep purple and patchouli, leached in long, grasping fingers from his pores. Could he smell her lust as well?

The music from the club oozed into her ears, bouncing around her brain. She visualized the notes swirling round in her head as his fingers danced over her sensitive flesh.

"My name is Lucien du Charmont," he hummed.

To her awakened senses, his voice sounded like chocolate, but tasted like marzipan. "I was born to nobility in the area known as Charmount, into the class of Noblesse d'eplée in the year 1761." The cadence of his voice was soft and dreamlike, like a bedtime story. Summer shut her eyes, allowing his voice to transport her to the countryside of eighteenth century France.

"My Chateau was a wide, white fortress of stone. Thirteen cerulean turrets stretched into the clouds above the great courtyard, where fine carriages and prancing horses clattered on limestone slabs."

So vivid was the vision that she truly seemed to be standing in the courtyard. The white chateau shimmered like the surface of the sea at sunset. Mullioned windows reflected a cloudless sapphire sky, while carriage wheels rolled across the stones with a gravelly grind. The rhythmic clip-clop of hooves carried her into a time in which she had never lived, but for this moment felt hauntingly familiar.

"It's so beautiful," she murmured.

"Yes, it was," he said wistfully. "Centuries before it came into my possession, it was the home of Catherine de Medici." Lucien drew a deep, melancholy breath. "As with most things, all was not as it appeared."

There was a nervous shifting in his posture - a prickle of tension crackling the air.

"My life was one of extreme indulgence and numerous excesses, a typical life of French nobles in those days. We considered it very chic, in fact, to show indifference to the less fortunate. We felt above the common rabble. I was spoiled and entitled. No one would have cried 'foul' if I had died at the hands of the peasant revolutionaries."

Summer envisioned the Lucien of long ago; fortunate and untroubled, exquisite in face and form with sun-streaked locks curled round his face and the flash of a devilish smile. It was with a heavy heart she realized that the devil-may-care young man was only a phantom now; his vibrant life-light extinguished by something or someone.

"One evening, while I was pursuing my favorite pastimes of whoring and drinking..." Lucien paused for a moment, and then continued, his voice snarled, "...the revolution came. I arrived home to see my manor ablaze with the fires of rebellion. Like an odious shroud, the stench of burning fleshes - animal and human - blanketed the air."

As the scene sprang to life in her mind's eye, an icy numbness spread through her chest, inching its way into her throat, bringing a feeling of total, utter helplessness. She sensed these were his emotions - the ones he'd experienced that dreadful night. So intense, so real were these feelings, she felt certain that he must carry them with him still.

"By the hair of their heads, my friends and family were dragged from their beds. I remember drawing my sword from its scabbard and charging up the stairs." Lucien stroked his fingers through her hair. "Alas," he said, his words a blend of old and new, which Summer found curious, as if he slipped between centuries like some time traveller, "being the drunken bastard that I was, I stumbled and fell, only to find a dozen dirty hands lifting me from the floor. They dragged me to where, in helpless horror, I was forced to watch the mob defile and shred my wife to a mass of unrecognizable blood and bone."

It seemed a sound caught in the vampire's throat - a small strangling thing - and then it was gone, but it left his voice as cracked and dry as the rustle of late autumn leaves. "They used my very own sword to hack her to bits."

The scene's horror was terrible. Summer tried forcing the images from her mind, the sorrow of the memory crushing her chest with the weight of a thousand cannonballs, and she struggled to fill her lungs with air.

"I failed to protect the ones that I loved most, and the guilt of this abomination consumed me. To live one minute more with these ghastly images was more than I could bear. I had walked through the valley of death and come out the other side, my sanity teetering on the edge of the abyss. I begged them to slay me, too."

Summer gazed at the vampire. He stared straight ahead, his eyes viewing something in the distance that only he could see.

"But in their hatred, they did not slay me. The revolutionaries dragged me through the rat infested sewers of Paris, and, in a fire-lit alcove, they brought me before a priest."

He looked at her, cocking one eyebrow. "I thought they brought me to him so I might make my final confession. They announced to the priest that I was an aristocratic swine and that I had requested death."

Lucien paused. Summer wanted to say something, anything that might be of comfort, but his face held a faraway look, so she kept her silence. "I can still recall the sickly pale eyes of the cleric as they pierced my flesh and examined my soul. 'Oh, you are such a beautiful and exquisite young boy,' he said to me. 'Why is it that you wish to die?'

I explained that I would rather be put to death than to live with the horror I had witnessed, and implored him to kill me any way he liked, but to please release me from this living death."

Summer silently observed the vampire. His ancient and wondrous eyes stared into the distance, his head tilted to one side, as if trying to remember a fragment of a dream that lay just out grasp.

"Lies and half-truths like falling ash have covered much of my past, so that even I can no longer discern what is truth from what is myth, but my Conversion I recall with crystal clarity.

'Drink,' the priest urged, slicing his flesh after feasting on mine. 'Drink and you shall forget,' he promised."

A low, ironic laugh rumbled in the vampire's throat. "Thou shall not lie," he said. "That was only one of many commandments the unholy priest would break religiously. I drank his foul blood, even as my own oozed from the wounds on my neck. But I did not forget. Instead, his malicious punishment ensured that I might *never* look forward to blotting out the memory of those hours of darkness in the merciful arms of death." Tears burned her eyes as she considered the weight of all of the pain, the sorrow, the horror and the guilt that he had borne for hundreds of years. She pitied him with her whole heart, although she was certain that he did not want; did not need her pity.

He drained his drink from the glass, swallowing lustily, as if his throat were very parched.

"He must have genuinely thought I was beautiful because it was twenty-odd years before he tired of me." "Please, no more," Summer pleaded. The awful details were too much to hear. Summer took his hand in hers, pressing it to her cheek. "I'm sorry, but I just can't hear anymore right now. To think that you actually lived it…" she broke off, her throat so tight it burned.

The vampire tipped her chin with his hand, peering into her eyes.

"It's alright, mon chére. Such a dreadful story I know, but it is my story and I wanted you to hear it. If I had tears, I would have shed enough to fill two oceans, and still it would change nothing." He gave her the briefest smile - like a swift caress. "It is what it is - and it was a very, very long time ago. I have tried to learn to live with it, and learn from it."

He pinched her chin between his fingers, turning her face from side to side. "Tsk, tsk, tsk," he clucked. "Your makeup is running all down your pretty face."

He swiped at her cheeks with a napkin. "I'm not very good at this," he frowned, dropping the napkin to his lap. "Why don't you take a minute to powder your nose? The ladies' room is right around the corner." He began to rise from the table. "I'll walk you there."

Summer stood up, waving for him to be seated. She wanted to be alone for a moment with her thoughts.

"No, I'm a big girl. I can manage," she deferred, brushing the tears with the back of her hand. "I'm sorry. I'm not usually one for crying."

Gathering her purse, she excused herself. While snaking her way through the crowd, she blinked her eyes, battling back more tears. The vampire's story had plucked a string in her heart, and the note rang desolate and forlorn, like the call of a whippoorwill at twilight.

She didn't weep as a rule. It made her feel weak and vulnerable. When she cried, she also had to pee, and she disliked public rest rooms even more than she did crybabies. Her emotions had run away with her, it seemed.

Fucking green fairy!

Lucien kept a watchful eye on her as she departed. A sting of remorse pricked at his mind. It hadn't been his intention to upset her so deeply, but he felt the keen blade of truth was necessary to excise any romantic illusions she might have about his life.

Now that he had shared it, the burden he carried felt lighter somehow.

He hadn't told anyone his story before … human or vampire… It had become too heavy a load to carry alone, and he sensed his mind breaking under the weight of it.

"Hello, Lucien," purred a feminine voice. "I haven't seen you around in a while."

Lucien knew it was Isabelle even before he looked. The scent of her wood-rose dusting powder was unmistakable. He looked her over—a red-haired devil in a green dress.

She sat down as if she'd been invited, and slithered uncomfortably near him.

Lucien recoiled. Summer's seat wasn't even cold before Isabelle slid into it. She reminded him of a troll lurking under a bridge, waiting for her moment to strike.

"Isabelle," he said, leaning as far from her as he could without falling from his seat. "You're in my personal bubble; could you back up a bit?"

She acted as if she hadn't heard, closing the space between them even more. He slid down the banquette until half his ass cheek was hanging off the side, but it put a small distance between him and the vampiress.

"Lucien, aren't you pleased to see me? I am pleased to see you, even though you are a rat bastard."

Pleased was not exactly the word he would have chosen. *Some mistakes you never stop paying for.*

"So, tell me Lucien, who's your new little pet? Are you planning to turn her or shall I?" The hair on the back of his neck bristled. He narrowed his eyes, focusing his perception and tried to read if there was seriousness to her threat.

Isabelle was grinning at him, displaying a row of perfect teeth and two pointed canines. She looked older than he remembered...harder. There was a cruelty to her thin, crimson smile. She'd lined her pale, golden eyes heavily with black kohl and had drawn her eyebrows with no arches, just two thin, upward slanted lines that looked like a pair of open trap doors. What had he ever seen in her, he wondered, as she blinked at him. She was sewer trash -cunning and ruthless. But then, as they say, we are what we eat.

It was actually insulting that this gutter-snipe was trying to intimidate him. In vampire years, she was considered "newly minted." He could crush her into a thousand pieces if he wanted to, and come out without a scratch.

"Sorry, you catty whore, no one is turning anyone into anything. Do you understand what I am saying to you, or am I going to have to express myself more clearly on the matter?" Lucian twisted her arm until she winced.

Isabelle banged the flat of her free hand on the table, the cutlery bouncing with a tinny clang. "She's a Perceiver, Lucien," she hissed. "You know how naturally her kind turns to hunting our kind! You bring her here and you endanger us all!"

Lucien fixed her with a chilly stare, increasing the crushing pressure on her arm. Her thin bones shuddered beneath his fingertips.

"This is perilous, my friend," she spat, struggling to break free of his grasp. "You had better watch your step, because some of the community doesn't see it quite the same as you. Not all of us are going to have our heads turned by your impish mortal lover."

He let Isabelle thrash a bit before releasing her arm.

"Pffft," she whistled through her teeth before mounting a haughty retreat.

Cunt. Fuck her and her "community". He had fared just fine without the protection of their numbers. He wasn't fearful of Summer or of *them*. In fact, he'd had his fill of them for one night.

He leapt from his seat, elbowing his way through the crowd. He spotted Summer ambling down the hall from the rest room, wobbling under the influence of the absinthe. Pinpricks of guilt needled his conscience. He'd been foolish to allow her to wander around on her own. He rushed to meet her, taking her by the arm.

"Let's get out of here," he shouted above the pounding music.

Curious Cravings

Back at the loft, Summer did indeed invite Lucien inside to view her collection of Verve jazz recordings. As Ella Fitzgerald crooned *That Old Black Magic*, she coaxed Lucien into a dance.

That old black magic has me in its spell...that old black magic that you weave so well.

Summer laughed at the irony. It did feel like a spell, this sense of being suspended in time when she was with him. There was no yesterday to regret and no tomorrow to fear. There was only the moment...a lovely eternal *Now*.

His flesh felt cool beneath her fingertips as she stroked them along the sharp line of his jaw. She could almost forget what he was, as her head reclined against his chest, the soft cadence of his heartbeat drumming into her ear. The scent of sandalwood rose from his skin, and she inhaled deeply, filling her head with the primeval, peppery aroma.

Lucien danced her towards the window as the music slowly faded to an end. He opened the drapes, revealing the glittering lights below. Locked in a silent embrace, they looked out onto the city, while the repetitive scratch of the old phonograph needle jumped across the record. Summer wondered if that was what Lucien's past was like for him...a needle stuck in a groove, replaying the horrible refrain repeatedly without end.

Thinking about his past, of the things she knew and the things she didn't, gave her the uneasy, woozy feeling of looking out over a ledge from a great height.

Lucien was so much more than she had first perceived him to be. More than the sum of his parts, an immortal and a mortal, who had once had a real life - who had known real love. A whisper of alarm rippled up her spine as she wondered if he was looking to love again...with her.

Surely, love between a mortal and an immortal could only end badly.

But making love - that was a subject she could wrap her legs around! She wasn't fool enough to think that she'd be his first human tryst, but she was a vampire virgin. Her head swam thinking about it.

"Be careful, mon petite," Lucien whispered. "When you are this close to me, I can read your thoughts."

Summer drew a sharp breath, wilting with embarrassment.

"It's not that I was trying," he explained running his hands over her arms, his touch as intoxicating as champagne bubbles. "I figured I should let you know, considering the direction your thoughts were taking."

He'd heard her thoughts, known she was thinking about making him her lover. Her cheeks burned with mortification.

"Don't be embarrassed," he soothed, petting her hair. "If you could read my thoughts right now, they would raise more than your eyebrows."

He grabbed her buttocks, and the squeeze gave her that runaway, teenage horny feeling. He pulled her body close to his, the shaft of his penis so rigid it felt as if he had a Billie club shoved in his pants.

"Can you tell what I am thinking right now?" she asked teasingly, her fingers playing over the buttons of his shirt.

He leaned over, his breath danced through the strands of her hair as he whispered in her ear. "Let me see…," a moment's pause, and then, "I have it now. What a dirty little girl. You are thinking about my cock," he scolded, his voice aghast with feigned shock.

It was true, he really could see into her mind. The knowledge that he possessed this power gave her the same feeling as a roller coaster ride, frightening and thrilling at the same time. Now she understood why Lois Lane went so ga-ga over Superman.

"Can all vampires read thoughts?" she asked.

"No," he replied. "We all have different talents, or combinations of them."

Her curiosity piqued and with thoughts of his cock momentarily put on the backburner, she probed to know more. "Such as?"

"Well," he said, rocking her in his arms. "There's vaporization - one of my favorites." The corners of his mouth turned up in a smile. "Somnambulism - I've never been much use at that. Shape shifting - that one I really don't see the need for when vaporization works just as well in most cases." He shrugged his shoulders, "Some seem to enjoy it, but to me it's just showing off."

Summer felt weak in the knees. "Anything else?'

"Many things," he nodded. "Time-bending; dominion over creatures; flight. Oddly, sometimes abilities just pop up that you didn't even know you had...or perhaps they grow with time...no one really knows."

"Hmmm," she hummed, half to herself and half out-loud, as she contemplated how these things were possible with the laws of physics, but she'd never had a good understanding of physics. Its concepts seemed a slippery thing, always wiggling from her mental grasp.

She supposed that unless she wanted to give herself a nasty headache, she'd simply have to learn to accept the validity of certain things without question.

"Now, where were we before we got sidetracked?" He nuzzled her ear, and it was as if the feet of a dozen centipedes skittered across her neck. "I remember now. I was just about to do this..."

His mouth descended on hers, the lusty fullness of his lips as plump and juicy as slices of warm apple. He tasted faintly of cinnamon and salt as his tongue played over hers. She slipped her hands up under the tail of his shirt to feel the cool firmness of his muscles, and his arms closed round her. Again, she felt the rigidness of his cock pressing low on her abdomen, and she longed to examine it with her fingers as one might some rare and extravagant treasure.

She sucked his tongue into her mouth, imagining his cock there instead, its head hard and round as a cue ball. Her hand went naturally to it, stroking him through the fabric of his trousers, her touch making him moan.

What did it look like, she wondered, her head spinning from curiosity and desire, the thin strip of her panties wet and warm between her legs. Was it as pale and as enchanting as his face?

Lucien's mind reeled - his desire to bed her overriding his judgment.

He'd seen them before...vampire groupies. Slavering little minions that trailed the undead, hoping to add another preternatural prick to their collection, not worrying if they'd survive to tell the tale. He had enjoyed his fair share...giving what they wanted, and taking what he deserved.

But Summer was different. He wanted her, but he wanted all of her. He didn't care to be an idle curiosity, discarded after a slap and a tickle.

"Summer," Lucien gasped. "Please stop, please."

He jerked his hips away from her touch, his hand stilling hers.

For a moment she thought maybe was going to come in his pants or something, but the look on his face when he pulled away, the knitted brow, the tenseness in his jaw, told her he was refusing her advances.

He averted his eyes from her glare and mouthed, "I'm sorry." "You gotta be kidding me, right?" Summer stared at him, her upturned palms begging for an explanation, her body itching with irritation while her mind swirled with confusion.

"It's not that I wouldn't love to take you up on your offer," he grasped her hands in his, both of his closing over both of hers. "It's just that I have some *concerns*."

Summer now fully understood the term, "Blow your mind" because that was exactly how she felt, as if the Roadrunner had planted one of those cartoon packs of dynamite in her brain and pushed the plunger. *He's the blood-sucking undead and yet he's the one with "concerns".*

"What kind of *concerns?*" she asked with a curl of her lip. "AIDS, herpes, warts, little fanged babies nine months from now?"

Releasing her hands, he walked to the sofa, taking a seat. Summer watched, mouth agape, as he propped his feet on the coffee table as if he owned the joint. He worked his fingers through his hair, the locks slipping through the spaces like strands of spider silk.

"My concerns are, that is to say," he foundered, "that it might be a pity or curiosity fuck, and I am not looking for either one," he said all in one breath.

Since her mouth was already open, her knee-jerk instinct was to shoot it off - to tell him how full of shit he was - but then she thought back on the things that had run through her mind and realized that he might have a point. The realization stung as smartly as a slap in the face.

"Please don't take it as an accusation," he said. "It's only because I've traveled that highway before and don't want you and me to be like that."

Summer needed a drink to help soak up his words. She crossed to the bar, pulled a bottle from the mirrored shelf and poured two tall ones, with a chaser of self-examination.

She *was* curious. How couldn't she be? The pity part - okay, she had to admit there might be a *sliver* of a savior complex mixed in with the sexual attraction.

"Fair enough," she declared, the ice cubes clinking softly against the crystal as she plunked them into the glass. "I'll admit that some of what you say could be at play here." She crossed the room, handing off one of the glasses to Lucien, and then stepping out of her shoes because they pinched her feet to distraction.

"It's not entirely pity, you know. I mean, have you looked in the mirror lately?"

Lucien rolled his eyes as in "can you really be that stupid?"

"My bad," she said, sheepishly shrugging. "What I meant to say was that you are very attractive, and I *am* only human."

"Anything else?" he asked.

"No," she replied. "One part pity, and two parts lust…that's about the sum of it."

"Curiosity." It was a statement not a question. While he sat there picking an imaginary piece of lint off of his trousers, Summer's tongue, uncertain how to respond, knotted up like a pretzel.

"Admit that you are curious about what it would be like to have sex with a vampire," he said, like a parent who already knows you broke the lamp, but won't be satisfied until you own up to it.

Summer chewed her bottom lip. What's the use, he already knows.

"Okay, I admit it. I am curious." Cocking her head to one side she asked, "Is it wrong? Isn't curiosity what drives most sexual encounters?"

Lucien raised an eyebrow. "Ah, you've found a loophole." He smiled.

"Come," he said, patting the sofa cushion, "sit next to me."

"No way," she said raising her hands, "I don't want to be accused of molestation."

She plopped on the table, beside his legs, doing her best not to notice how his trousers hugged the curve of his thigh the way the Coastal Highway hugged the Pacific shore.

"I'll sit right here if that's alright with you."

"Aww, mon petite, don't be angry." He leaned forward, squeezing her knee. "I don't want us to make a mess of things. I want more from you than sex, although I am sure that when it happens it will be very nice." He leaned back against the sofa. "Only it won't be tonight."

In a weird way, she felt relieved, and she knew it was relief because that tense little knot in her chest that she hadn't even known existed was conspicuous by its absence.

"Relax, Lucien…I get where you're coming from," she said, knocking his knee playfully with hers. "My pride was just a bit wounded, but I'm over it."

She *was* over it…for the most part.

Lucien stretched the weariness from his bones, and then balanced the back of his head on his interlaced fingers. It had been a long night and that prickly restlessness had begun.

"You're kind of a lonely guy, aren't you?" she asked, aquamarine eyes peering out from behind a lush fringe of lashes.

Does it show that much?

"I suppose I am," he agreed, feeling too weary for talk, but grateful for the companionship tonight. He felt as if he lived in a state of eternal winter, but a few hours with her, and he could almost remember what it was like to know the sun upon his face.

He didn't feel much like talking anymore. He held his arms out, inviting her in. She came to him - just that easy - came to him without fear, curling into his lap and melting unquestioningly into his arms. Such a small thing; but a miracle all the same.

"You don't see me as a horrible thing, do you?" he asked.

Summer uncurled her legs, crossing one knee over the other. He smelled the dampness from beneath her skirt and wondered what pleasures might await him in her secret, hidden places.

"No, of course not," she said, her fingers tracing small, slow circles on his chest.

Sweet, sweet girl.

"After centuries of only being seen as some terrible thing, you begin to believe it yourself." He cupped her chin with his hand, tipping her face towards his. "Do you understand what I mean?"

She exhaled a long sigh, blue eyes behind batting lashes like flashing neon. "I'm trying to."

"Am I the monster others believe me to be? I need to find out, you see?" He frowned at her, playfully. "Maybe I'm a little afraid to know the answer. As the song goes, 'Fifty million Frenchmen can't be wrong.'"

She slipped her arms around his waist, snuggling her head on his shoulder, her scent, tuberose and lemongrass, hovering like a hummingbird around her head.

Beneath the translucent skin of her neck, Lucien eyed the pulse of her jugular vein, as inviting as the blinking light of an all-night diner. Like a starving dog, hunger chewed on his bones. The mortals he fed on were so full of despair and self-loathing that each time he drank from them, he felt made over until their wretchedness seemed to ooze from his very pores.

The temptation of ingesting the life-force of one with so much vivaciousness and passion as she possessed was dizzying. The power of those magical cells would be a tonic for his miserable soul. He closed his eyes and imagined drinking from her, her corpuscles coursing through his veins, quickening him with vitality that grew in intensity with each mouthful. He saw his mouth clamped to her neck, feasting on her as if she were Christmas dinner, slaking his thirst with her last drop of precious fluid, his body and soul ablaze with her energy. He quaked at the thought. Then he saw her limp, bloodless form lying in his arms and he trembled with horror and loathing.

Sickened by his thoughts, a bitter taste filled his mouth. He had to leave this place before his vision became a reality. He had gone too long without feeding and his mind was mad with hunger.

"I-I have to be going," he stammered, placing his feet on the floor. Summer slipped from his lap. "You're leaving?" she asked, her eyes entreating, her lips so inviting.

"It's nearly dawn. I need to feed," was all he said. He had no time for long goodbyes. He strode towards the elevator and pulled back the iron grating. It made a sound like chattering teeth.

Summer put her hand over the button that signaled the elevator door to open. "Let me come with you."

Blasphemy! His stomach recoiled with the force of a Glock .45 ACP. Hadn't he given her enough visions of horror for one night?

"No, never - I will not place that burden on you!" He peeled her fingers from the button and pressed it. The doors opened with a clatter and groan. He locked his eyes on her and set his jaw. "Please do not ever ask this of me again."

He knew she must think him mad, as she stood there with her arms folded, looking confused as hell. But he'd not eaten for three days and her blood smelled to him like a sizzling steak.

His words had come out harsh. It was the Beast talking, snapping at his mind. He didn't want to leave this way, so he cradled her face in his hands, and put his mouth on hers, his tongue probing for one last taste. Her lips were warm and moist; he lost himself, his passion and gnawing hunger spiraling with each sigh of her body. The two needs battled inside of him as he crushed her mouth with his, stumbling her to the wall with a thud.

The burn of her fingernails raked his back as he ground his hips into hers. He wanted to pound his cock into her with the same manic urgency that hunger pounded through his veins. She wrapped one leg around his thigh, grappling him with a lusty groan. The heat crawled from between her legs as he thrust his hips into her with such determination it caused something on the wall above their heads to crash to the floor.

From the corner of his eye, he glanced to see what it was. A broken clock lay at his feet, its hands frozen at five thirty-two.

He could not risk tarrying another moment.

"I have to go," he said, his voice as dry as his veins. Summer nodded her head in agreement. "I know," she panted. "Tomorrow night, then?" Summer touched her fingers to her brow thoughtfully as if collecting her thoughts. "Um, I'm booked for a personal appearance around eight tomorrow night, but I'll be free after that. How should I contact you?" Laughing he said, "Don't worry, Mon chére, I'll find you... à tout à l'heure."

The Wangdangdoodle

The garish pink-sparkle billboard along I-70 announced the entrance to the gravel parking lot of Bottoms Up Fetish Emporium. Summer parked her car at the rear entrance of the long, low pole building; a cloud of dust trailing her tires.

"The things I do to pay the bills," she sighed, looking at the billboard.

Inside the store, Summer was assaulted with the sight of canes, crops, chainmail, clamps, collars, gags, floggers, and mysterious items meant for mysterious uses. *I might have to do a little shopping before I leave here today.*

"Summer, you made it!" Good old reliable Melody was waiting, and had already set up for the appearance. Summer broke into a broad smile and scurried to the table that served as central command for the night. She enjoyed doing remotes, and it was always a kick doing them with Melody.

"Okay, here are the T-shirts for you to sign." Melody held up a powder blue t-shirt with 'Only the Lonely' emblazoned across the front.

Summer surveyed the tees with a critical eye, nodding her head in approval. They were cute. The printer had done a nice job.

"I have tons of Sharpies too, so you don't run out of ink, and here are the ballots and ballot box for the KJZM prize promotion. Don't worry about those; I will make sure everyone fills them out properly."

"Wow, Mel, thanks so much for doing all of this. I can always count on you to come through for me." Summer smiled.

"We are going live with the promo in thirty seconds. Here's your copy to read, and I see some of your listeners are already coming through the door."

Summer took her seat at the microphone; the little buzz of adrenaline that she felt when going live zipped through her system. Men and women of all shapes and ages queued up for the meet and greet.

Cradling the mike in her hands, she breathily announced, "Good evening, listeners. This is Summer Solstice coming to you live from the Bottoms Up Fetish Emporium on I-70, just west of St. Louis. I will be here for the next two hours, so come on out and snag a free 'Only the Lonely' T-shirt, and be sure to sign up for KJZM's prize giveaway extravaganza.

"While you are here, don't forget to check out Bottoms Up's new line of leather fetish gear, featuring the smoking hot collection of Backdraft Assless Chaps."

Summer smiled approvingly at the totally tasteless product name.

"Mention KJZM and receive ten percent off of your purchase for the next two hours. It looks like the lines are forming, so I will return you to Chattin' about Chicks with Crockett and Tubbs."

"Until the next commercial break, this is Summer Solstice, broadcasting live from Bottoms Up Fetish Emporium, right next to St. Louis' newest Gentlemen's Club: The Twattery Barn."

Summer was biting her lips to keep from laughing at the name of the club. Turning off her mike, Summer spied Melody trying just as hard not to crack, and they both broke into a fit of giggles.

"Don't you just love it when the new Twattery Barn catalog arrives in the mail?" Melody squealed.

"Hi, Summer. Would you sign a t-shirt for me?" An uneasy gentleman sporting a swirling comb-over interrupted their joking. Summer composed herself, wiping the tears of laughter from her eyes. "Sure, honey, what's your name?" She uncapped a marker while Melody handed her a shirt.

"Adam, my name is Adam." "OK, here you go, Adam," Summer signed her name and handed him the T-shirt. Melody shoved a square of paper into his outstretched hand.

"Don't forget to sign up for KJZM's prize extravaganza!" Melody chimed in with surprising enthusiasm. Melody was many things, but chipper wasn't usually one of them.

Aww, Summer thought, *she's taking one for the team.*

For over an hour, the scene repeated: Summer cheerfully signed shirts, Melody pretended to be excited about handing out entry ballots, and Summer took it all in stride when the occasional fan lewdly came on to her. A few wanted her to sign their underwear, or various body parts, and she congenially obliged them - within limits. All in a day's work. "Hi, Summer, I'm Jerry, remember me?"

He was munching on a donut and the powdered sugar peppered his faded, food stained, 1979 Cher 'Take Me Home' tour cotton shirt which stretched over his pot belly like Saran-wrap on a matzo ball. A pager and cell phone, which Summer expected never rang, hung from his double knit, security guard issue trousers. His body odor was as ripe as hobo taint.

"Does a banker remember a bad check?" Summer couldn't forget Jerry if she tried. He attended all of her outside gigs. He was like a pesky little brother that followed her around, wanting to hang out with the cool kids, but he was devoted to her and always available to lend a hand breaking down the sets after a remote.

"Here you go, Jerry," said Summer, handing him a T-shirt. "Try not to get any food stains on it."

"Thanks, Summer. Mind if I hang around? I could help Melody hand out the entries?"

"Sure, Jerry, knock yourself out," she said, dismissing him with a wave of her hand.

A small pudgy man, with the complexion of library paste, restlessly shifted his weight from one foot to the other, waiting his turn in line. His eyes darted about like a frightened bird, stealing nervous glances over his shoulder as he stepped up to the table.

Summer reached for a shirt to sign. "Who should I make this out to?" A barely audible "Bob" squeaked from the man's mouth. "You can make it out to Bob. I talked to you on Friday night, but you probably don't remember me."

He was wrong, Summer remembered him. She remembered him well.

"I'm the one that sees vampires, and I need to ask you something," Bob whispered. "There's a guy over there, by the dildos...don't let him see you looking...I think he's a vampire."

Summer casually surveyed the room, her eyes coming to rest on a man with his back to her. He was examining a device called The Invader. A blue flame hovered faintly over his head. As if sensing eyes on him, the vampire turned in her direction.

Lucien - it was Lucien. Biting the inside of her cheeks, she consciously turned the corners of her mouth into a frown as she tried to restrain the grin of recognition pulling at her face. Her heart beat with the giddiness of a schoolgirl.

"Do you see him, Summer?" Bob hissed. "Does he look like a vampire to you?"

"Sorry, Bob," she consoled, "I think you're wrong this time. I just see a regular guy - holding a *frighteningly* enormous dildo - no vampires in here tonight."

Leaning across the table she whispered, "There's nothing to be afraid of here, Bob. You are safe…well, as safe as you can be in a fetish emporium on a major interstate. Now, here's your T-shirt, and be sure to sign up for the giveaway."

With a furtive glance in Lucien's direction, Bob snatched his T-shirt, hurriedly filled out the entry and bolted out of the door. "Weirdo," Melody contended. "If that gorgeous hunk of fuck-meat is a vampire, he can suck on me anytime that he wants. Melody hitched her thumb in Lucien's direction. "Check him out, Summer," she urged. Melody placed her elbows on the table, her chin resting in her hand. Her eyes gazed dreamily at Lucien. "If I ever got my hands on that guy, I'd strap him down and show him what this tongue stud is for." She waggled her tongue suggestively, showing off the round steel ball embedded in it. Summer thumbed through commercial scripts trying to appear unimpressed, but Melody was unstoppable.

"I'd give him a hot roll with cream." Her foot tapped rapidly on the floor.

"Do the mommy-daddy dance…" She performed a little "Oh yeah" dance in her seat. "Take a poke in the ole cat whiskers -"

"I get it!" Summer interrupted irritably. "He churns your butter! Now cool it," she hissed. "He's walking this way."

Summer straightened her spine and smiled sweetly in Lucien's direction. Christ, he was gorgeous. Melody was right; Summer wouldn't mind taking a poke in the ole cat whiskers from him either.

"Would you be so kind as to autograph my Wangdangdoodle?" Lucien implored, proffering a blue jelly dildo complete with rotating ball bearing beads and squeezable testicles.

"I would *love* to sign your Wangdangdoodle. Would you like me to sign it right here or should we step outside?" Summer flirted.

Melody kicked her sharply on the shin. Summer impaled Melody with a 'back off' glare.

"I'd really be pleased if you would sign my Wangdangdoodle right here…in front of all of these people," he said. "Holy shit," Melody drawled with her attention fixated on their interaction.

Summer tried not to laugh. It was nearly impossible to appear indifferent to Lucien when she felt like melting into his arms.

"Whatever you say, cowboy," countered Summer, holding out her hand. Lucien slapped the dildo into her palm and her fingers closed around the shaft. It felt so realistic in her hand…firm, but slightly spongy with rigid raised veins. Her mind wandered to the unknown wonder of Lucien's prick, and her hand tightened around the rubber cock.

"I don't think I caught your name," Summer teased, caressing the Wangdangdoodle with her hands.

"Just make it out to Matteo, like the Café Matteo on the riverfront. Do you know the place?"

Summer's pulse quickened at the reference to their rendezvous.

"That cozy little café, that doesn't open until eleven o'clock at night? Yes, I know exactly where you mean," she conspired. How cleverly he had worked their meeting spot into the conversation.

"There you go," she twittered.

The Wangdangdoodle slipped from her hand as she offered it to Lucien, launching into the air and bouncing on the carpet. "Whoops," she cried. Lucien and Summer simultaneously dived to the floor as they followed the bouncing dildo.

Crouching on the floor, Lucien whispered, "I'll meet you at eleven, in front of Matteo's." With a wink, he recovered his autographed Wangdangdoodle and departed into the night.

Smoothing her skirt, Summer implored, "Mel, are we almost finished here? I have to find a ladies room."

"Yeah, we're done. That hottie with the loaf of French bread rising in his pants was the last in line."

Summer broke into a quick stride towards the rest room, in a hurry to wrap things up. Her vampire waited.

"Wait up; I'll go with you," Melody called out, scurrying after her. "Jerry can clean up until I get back, can't you, Jerry?"

"Sure, sure…I'll take care of things. Where do you want all of this stuff to go?"

"Just throw it in my car, will you, Jerry?" Summer tossed her car keys at him.

"Sure, Summer, I can do that for you."

***

"Okay, Summer, spill it - what was up between you and Frenchy out there?" Melody demanded, her voice echoing from inside the bathroom stall.

"Nothing, just some friendly flirting." Summer leaned towards the mirror, wiping lipstick from the corners of her mouth with the tip of her finger.

"Fuck-me-running, Summer! That's bullshit and you know it. I could practically feel the chemistry between you two."

Did it show that much? She examined her face for tell-tale signs. Her reflection stared back at her accusingly.

"I wish," she sighed, trying her best to sound genuine.

"I saw him first, bitch," Melody joked. "If anyone is going to Napoleon his Bonaparte, it's going to be yours truly."

"Oh, that's a good one, Melody - very clever." She felt the urge to tell her; the words were on the tip of her tongue. She was dying to tell someone! The funny thing about a secret was the longer you kept it, the larger it seemed to grow, and this particular secret was ballooning so fast, she felt it might pop from her mouth like a cork from a champagne bottle. But there was no time, and this totally wasn't the place. She decided to keep her secret for another day.

"Well, have at it, girl, he's all yours!"

"Yeah, fat chance after he got a look at you." Melody punctuated her remark with a flush of the toilet. "I'm going to meet some friends, wanna come along?"

"Thanks, but I think I'll just go home and watch a movie or something. I'm not really in the going out mood."

"Whatever works for you. See you tomorrow night at the station."

Summer tossed her head back, staring at the ceiling tiles and heaved a deep sigh of relief. That was a close one.

As she swung open the rest room door, she nearly knocked Jerry unconscious.

"I'm sorry, Summer," he stammered. "I was just waiting to return your car keys. Do you want me to walk you to your car?"

Uh…No! Summer's skin prickled. How long had he been standing outside the door? Was Creepy McCreeperson listening to their conversation? Summer just wanted rid of him so she could speed down the highway towards her vampire.

"No, Jerry, I think I can manage. It's parked just outside the door."

"Okay, Summer, I put everything on the floor in the back. I hope that's alright." "Perfect. Jerry, listen, I have to get going." "Okay, I'll call you tomorrow, Summer!"

Down by the River

Her shoes made a crunching sound on the loose gravel as she walked along the deserted riverfront road. Eleven o'clock on a Sunday night was not exactly prime time down by the river.

Anxious to meet up with Lucien, she decided to take a shortcut by ducking into Clamorgan Alley, where she caught one of her heels in the cobblestones. When she stopped to check her shoe, a faint sound of footsteps echoed in the distance. She turned her ears to the night air. The only sound was the distant rumble of thunder from the threatening sky. She looked down the length of the alley behind. It was empty, save for a ginger cat padding noiselessly on the hunt.

She could have sworn that she heard someone walking behind her.

These old streets had a way of playing tricks on your ears, though. Sounds bounced off of the tall brick buildings like pinballs. Still, she couldn't shake the eerie feeling as she headed toward Morgan Street.

There it was again; someone keeping pace with her steps. When she stopped, they stopped. When her pace quickened, so did the phantom footsteps.

She considered breaking into a run, but what or whom was she running from? Summer paused mid-stride and glanced furtively over her shoulder, where she came face to scowling face with the Vicious Ones. Dodger, Marcus, Nitro and Gaston formed a wall of vampires across the narrow alley.

She gasped, clamping her hand to her heart to keep it from bursting through her chest. Her legs, like two logs of Jell-o quivered and quaked. A cloud of air, so cold it set her teeth to chattering, passed through her like a ghost in a graveyard.

Shit, what is this about? Summer shot a quick glance at her surroundings. No one in sight for the entire length of the alley - she was on her own.

The vampires maintained their distance, neither advancing nor retreating. They stood shoulder to shoulder, arms crossed and legs spread into a wide stance. Summer raced through her options. Running was futile. You can't outrun lightning. She could scream, but who was there to hear? Only one choice left.

"What do you boys want?" she challenged.

"Funny, we were wondering the same thing of you," Nitro sneered.

"Yes, Perceiver," growled Marcus. "We would like you to explain what you were doing in our bar playing footsies with Lucien?"

"Now, fellas pull your fangs in," Summer replied, with a confidence that she didn't feel. "I'm not out to do you any harm. We just stopped in for a drink, nothing more."

"It looked like you two had more in mind than quenching your thirst," sniffed Dodger, with a toss of his glossy black hair. "Tell us, do you really imagine that a vampire could even be remotely interested in you as more than a meal? I assure you, your relationship is quite impossible and ill-advised." The rest of the gang snickered in agreement.

Summer's gut roiled with irritation. Anger rose in her like mercury in a thermometer on an August night. What business was it of theirs what she did? Nosey little fuckers.

"Who said anything about a relationship?" Summer questioned. "We're just having some kicks. I'm sure you know what that's like. Now if you fellows are finished…"

"We're not!" bellowed Nitro, stopping her in her tracks, her shoulders jerking at the sound. "If this is just an infatuation, then end it!"

Without detection, he had instantly, silently moved closer. His dark eyes, large and black as a crow's, peered narrowly at her. Summer stumbled backward, gulping at the terror which clawed at her throat.

"I suggest that you find another way to get your kicks," he sneered. "Did he tell you that you're special?"

Summer's cheeks burned with heat. She wanted to shrink inside of herself and disappear.

"Oh, you're special all right - this week's special, that is - the soup du jour." The vampires burst into a chorus of mocking laughter.

They didn't understand…could never understand. Fucking schoolyard bullies!

The whole of her spine was trembling, but she set her jaw, her indignation bubbling to the surface. Enough was enough.

"Are you finished?" she challenged.

"One more thing," Dodger leered. "If you need to save someone, Perceiver, save yourself. Consider yourself warned." Just like that, they turned in unison, and stomped towards Washington Avenue. Summer exhaled, covering her mouth with quivering hands. A wave of exhaustion flowed over her, as the tenseness in her muscles retreated.

She leaned against the building, trying to wrap her mind around the encounter. She wasn't sure if it was a warning, a threat, or both. They had called her Perceiver. Was her ability that much of a menace to them? Did they assume she had some sinister motive for being with Lucien?

Lucien. She could tell him about this but what good would it do? Either he would be angered and do God knows what to them, or he would confirm their allegations about him. She found both options unappealing.

Still fuming from her confrontation with the Vicious Ones, Summer rounded the corner. Lucien leaned against the wall of Café Matteo, a cigarette dangling from his mouth. Smoke rose in ribbons above his head, evaporating into the damp night air. He appeared healthier and less agitated than he had last night. Summer wondered if he had recently fed.

"If it isn't old Wangdangdoodle," she quipped. "In the flesh, squeezable testicles and all," Lucien spread his arms out to receive her. "You have little goose bumps all down your arms. Are you cold, mon petite?" He removed his jacket and placed it on her shoulders. "There now, better?"

Summer nodded. She wasn't truly cold. The episode in Clarmorgan Alley was still with her. She had been warned, but against what? If they were trying to frighten her away from Lucien, that was a warning that she had no intention of heeding.

She was careful to shield her thoughts from Lucien. *Think about something else…baseball…new shoes…the Wangdangdoodle…anything.*

"Let's walk a while, shall we?" His arm around her waist, Lucien guided her down to the river's edge. The wind stirred, kicking up small waves and rocking the docked boats against their moorings. A gentle rain began to fall, the drops making a plopping sound as they pinged off the surface of the water.

"So much for our romantic stroll," Summer shrugged. "What now?" Lucien looked to the right and the left. "There!" He pointed to a highway overpass several hundred yards away. "Let's make a run for it." As the rain turned from gentle to driving, it filled Summer's shoes and plastered her white silk shirt against her skin. Chilled to the bone but with a heart lighter than air, she ran through the deluge with Lucien, jumping puddles and skipping around the rivulets that snaked down the levee on their way to the river. Breathless, their drenched bodies stumbled into the welcome refuge of the leaky overpass.

"Hmm, I wonder how long this will last," Summer lamented, as sheets of rain washed down onto the bricks and cascaded over the levee into the muddy waters of the Mississippi.

"Who can tell? Only God knows such things. But at least we have this leaky roof over our heads, and ..." Lucien searched the jacket around Summer's shoulders, producing a bottle of French wine and a corkscrew. "We have wine. Sorry, no glasses, we will have to chug it from the bottle."

"Lucien," she teased in her best Southern belle accent, batting her lashes with Scarlet O'Hara precision. "You take me to all the nicest places! First that lovely, rat-infested alleyway, and now this! Glory be, you do know how to turn a girl's head!"

"Oh!" he cried, putting his hand over his heart feigning injury. "Your sharp tongue has struck a mortal wound to my manly pride."

Summer laughed. She adored Lucien when he was light hearted and joking. In moments like this, Summer completely forgot that he was a vampire. It all seemed so normal. Maybe it was. It wasn't more than a few decades ago when people thought interracial relationships were perverse; now most knew differently. But what about inter-species? That term wasn't technically correct. Lucien wasn't a different species. Was he?

"Ladies first," he put the bottle to her lips. She took a small sip. "Go on, more, more," he urged. "It will help to warm you."

Lucien tilted the bottle higher, and she drank deeply of the sweet garnet liquid. It trickled down her throat, through her chest, and pooled in her empty stomach filling her with a cozy feeling.

Lucien put his mouth on hers, licking the juice which clung to her lips. She tasted its sweet flavor on his tongue.

"Delicious," she declared, wiping her mouth.

"Delightful," he teased, cupping her breast into his hand through the sodden silk of her shirt.

Summer didn't care—vampire or man—she desired Lucien more than she desired anyone she had ever known. She unbuttoned her blouse, peeling it away from her body, and urged his mouth to her breast.

He pounced on her, his lips warm against her rain-soaked flesh, and his tongue traced scorching circles around her puckered nipple. She swooned, her body wilting like a daisy in the noonday sun.

Taking him by the hair, she yanked his head back and hungrily fixed her eyes on his. "That feels so fucking good," she snarled from between clenched teeth.

He grabbed her wrists, imprisoning her arms against the wall. She squealed with delight, reveling in the sensation of his domination as he ravaged her tits, panting and growling like a jackal.

The sky continued to shower torrents. Jagged bolts of lightning lit up the black sky, illuminating the tunnel with ghostly green flashes.

Summer heard the low rumble of thunder, but was it in the atmosphere or pounding in her veins?

He pressed his cheek to hers. Shivers tickled the back of her neck as his breath blew across her ear. "What do you want?" he whispered.

Summer knew with the utmost certainty what she wanted. She wanted this half-man, half-monster to fuck her like the beast he was. She wanted to experience the ravages of his passion, unbridled and without restraint. She wanted him to pound her against the wall of the leaking tunnel until her body was bruised and wracked.

Summer grabbed his belt buckle and yanked him against her, feeling the jolt of their bodies colliding all the way down her spine.

"I want you to fuck me, Lucien. Fuck me like an animal!"

Summer ripped open his belt, the clang of the metal buckle echoing in the tunnel. Then she unzipped his trousers. The vampire's sizeable prick stretched his boxer briefs to the seams.

Hooking her pinky onto the waistband, she tugged it away from his skin, while snaking her other hand down Lucien's abdomen and inside of his briefs, where her manicured fingers closed around his quivering cock.

A sharp intake of breath hissed between Lucien's teeth as she savored the steely hardness in her hand.

"See, I still have all the parts that I was born with," he said, sliding his cock through her fist.

He certainly did, and she wanted to feel this particular part ramming her very wet pussy. It didn't matter that they were soaked from the downpour. It didn't matter that they were in a polluted city underpass. Consumed with lust for the vampire, she cared only about the relentless hunger of her body for him.

Summer released his straining cock from its confines. It appeared much the same as any phallus, but there were aspects about it that she felt were far superior. The skin of Lucien's prick was as smooth and solid as a slab of marble—no wrinkles or folds—just taut, silky skin stretched over rigid blue veins, as if it had been chiseled from alabaster by a Renaissance master.

Lucien hiked her skirt above her hips and ran his hands up her inner thigh. Welcoming his touch, she opened her legs inviting him to come inside. When he grasped at her cunt through her panties, it was a long-awaited answer to her prayer. Even though it had only been a few days, she felt she had yearned an eternity for his touch on her sex. Summer shuddered and gasped as his hand dipped inside of her panties, spearing her with two fingers.

She rode his digits, the clink-clink of her silver bracelets bouncing off the walls of the tunnel as her hand stroked his shaft with a matching pace.

Craving, hot and demanding, raged through her body and brain as his fingers worked their wicked magic on her willing cunt. His fingers dipped in and out of her, smearing her clit with her own juices. She had never wanted a fucking so badly in her whole life.

"Do you have protection?" she panted. Lucien laughed, his fangs flashing in the light of the violent storm that surged around them. "Summer, I am not alive; nothing can live inside of me."

The idea of his unsheathed, unholy cock inside of her was almost more than she could bear. It was as if she was no longer flesh and blood. She was nothing but a swirling mass of white-hot desire.

"Take them off, then," she demanded. "Take them off - my panties - take them off." "May I tear them?" he asked. His eyes locked onto hers, his chest panting with anticipation.

"To shreds, Lucien. Tear them to shreds."

Lucien ripped the satin from her skin like a Band-Aid. Summer felt like a moth bursting free of a cocoon. Lucien's hand shot between her thighs, grasping at her pussy, his fingers gliding over her folds and clitoris, spreading silky lubrication over her sex.

"Oh, God, Lucien…"

"Please, not another fucking word," he demanded.

Sweeping her feet from the ground, he wrapped her legs around his hips and sunk his preternatural penis into her.

Summer's muscles clutched him as he fucked her. She bucked like an unbroken mustang to meet his thrusts.

It was all passion and frenzy - this first coupling - as two forces of nature came together to form a cataclysmic event.

They mated in the relentless rain. Summer dug her nails into Lucien's sinewy spine. He buffeted her against the stone wall, lacerating the delicate fabric of her white blouse. The deafening boom of rolling thunder drowned out her shrieks of pleasure.

Summer cradled her face in Lucien's neck, eyes squeezed tightly shut. She wanted to block out all of her other senses and concentrate only on her lustful organ.

The slap-slapping sound of their bodies resounded in the dark tunnel. Her orgasm rumbled in the distance, growing ever stronger, ever closer. Like an old friend, she welcomed the familiar twitching and clenching of her muscles - then a deluge, like a warm spring cloudburst, rained from her loins.

"I'm coming…oh, fuck, don't stop… I'm coming," she yowled.

Her hands clutched Lucien's buttocks. She rode his prick, pounding her throbbing clit against his pubic bone until her whole body jerked and trembled once more with sweet release. Lucien shuddered and growled, slamming her against the wall; spearing her with one last violent thrust of his prick, his slippery nectar oozing hotly down her thigh.

Requiem for the Lonely

The telephone's insistent ringing jolted Summer from her sleep.

Summer pushed her sleep mask onto her forehead, and squinted at the caller ID. The call was coming from Melody's cell phone.

She was so drowsy it seemed like she had only been sleeping a few hours. Had she overslept?

She sat bolt upright in bed, trying to get her bearings. The phone rang on unanswered. Rubbing her eyes, she peered out the window. The sky was once more raining down upon the city, blocking out the rays of the sun. A glance at the alarm clock reassured Summer that it was still midday.

She placed the receiver to her ear and slid back down under the covers.

"Hmmm…Melody, this had better be important," she mumbled, her eyelids fluttering towards sleep again.

"Summer, turn on the TV! Turn it to Channel 5," Melody shrieked.

Shit, fuck, shit! What the hell is this about? Summer fumbled blindly in her bedside drawer for the remote. Where was that damn thing?

"Mel, can I call you back? I can't find the damn remote. I need to reiterate, this had better be important. I was up very late last night."

"This is serious, Summer! Just hurry. I'm going to hang up and watch the newscast. Call me!"

Searching for the remote, she wondered what had Melody so worked up this time. Her irritation growing with each passing second, she recalled a previous time Melody had phoned with an urgent demand to turn on the news, only to end up watching some story about a "love doll" hump bitch for un-castrated canines that Melody thought was hilarious enough to disturb her sleep.

"There you are, you elusive little electronic device." Summer dug the remote out from where it was wedged between the headboard and the mattress. Arranging the pillows behind her back, she turned on the news report.

"Police are not yet saying if they suspect foul play." The on-the-spot reporter, Julia Lovewell, was shivering, her anorexic frame swallowed up inside of a yellow slicker.

Her backdrop was a foggy view of the riverfront. Police, ambulances and reporters swarmed the soggy scene. The wind from the storm buffeted her microphone, and sodden ropes of blond hair lashed her face and mouth as she spoke.

"They have identified the body as one Robert Spedinski of Creve Couer."

Tragic, Summer thought, yawning dismissively, but why the hell did Melody think it was okay to wake her from a sound sleep for it?

Reporter Lovewell placed a French-manicured nail to her ear, pressing at her earpiece, and then nodded her head.

"Right… if you are just joining us, I am Julia Lovewell reporting live for KBST, from the scene of a gruesome discovery.

"Early this morning, riverboat casino personnel spotted the body of a man floating near the riverboat with his leg tangled in rope. Witnesses described the man to be a white male, approximately five foot six, perhaps thirty-five years of age, and wearing a blue t-shirt emblazoned with 'Only the Lonely', a logo from a popular late night talk radio show, featuring host, Summer Solstice."

The sound of her name jolted Summer from half-sleep to full attention. *What the fuck?* Those tees were brand new - brought out for the first time yesterday. She had given out so many of them…dozens! She frantically searched her memory. What did they say that man's name was? Roger? No, Robert! She sat upright in her bed, her mind reeling.

Transfixed upon the television with her mouth agape, she felt the remote slip limply from her hand. The words were penetrating her ears, but her brain did not believe what she hearing.

"Julia," The cameras switched to split screen; Julia Lovewell and the riverfront spectacle on the right, and news anchor, Bryan McMannish, to the left. "Do you know if anyone has contacted Ms. Solstice?"

Contacted Ms. Solstice? What the fuck? Panicking, she turned off her telephone. *What in the hell do they think I know about this?*

"Bryan, no one here has mentioned if anyone has contacted Ms. Solstice yet."

"Julia, we are going to break away from the scene for a moment, because we have, in our studio, someone who says that they knew the deceased, and they have some very curious personal details about Robert Spedinski to relate."

A close-up of a pickle-puss woman in her late sixties replaced Julia Lovewell's image. Her haughty posture exposed her sense of self-importance.

"We have with us in the studio, the victim's neighbor, Joanne Buttner. What can you tell us about Robert, Ms. Buttner?"

"Mrs., it is Mrs. Buttner - well, Bob - everyone called him Bob…"

"Oh no," Summer croaked to the empty room. She suddenly felt very cold. Wrapping the blankets tightly around her, she silently prayed; *Please, oh please; don't let it be that Bob!*

The pinched-faced woman pursed her lips and continued, "Bob was a strange man. He kept to himself, mostly. I'm not sure what kinds of things he was into, exactly, but once I stopped by his apartment because I had locked myself out and needed to use his phone…" Mrs. Buttner took control of the microphone from the anchor's hand, looking straight into the camera and pausing for dramatic effect.

"God, everyone has to have their fifteen minutes of fame. Get on with it, you old bag," Summer bellowed at the TV.

"And, mind you, he had all of this disturbing vampire stuff; posters, books, newspaper clippings. I have to tell you, I made my phone call and got the heck out of there. It was creepy. I think that he might have been one of them devil worshipers."

Oh, my God! It is the same Bob! Summer's eyes burned as she blinked back tears of shock. Cold, creeping fear chilled her body. It invaded her stomach and pressed on her chest. The icy terror clawed at her throat, strangling her as she tried to dam back the lump forming in her windpipe.

Patting the nightstand with her hand, her eyes glued to the television, she picked up a pack of cigarettes. Damn. Empty. Swinging her feet to floor, she walked into her kitchen to retrieve a fresh pack, and turned on the gas burner to light a cigarette. Taking a deep breath, she opened the drapes and looked out upon the city. From her vantage point, she could make out flashing lights and figures in slickers working the scene. She turned on the living room television. The talking heads of KBST continued to report, as she watched the rain plummeting to earth.

"Did Mr. Spedinski have any enemies that you know of?" Bryan probed.

"Enemies? That man didn't even have any friends! I can't imagine how he would have had any enemies." Joanne Buttner stuck her nose in the air, striking a superior pose. "If you ask me, I think he just up and killed himself. I've never seen a man so isolated." Her pudgy fingers reached for control of the microphone again, but McMannish swung it out of her reach in the nick of time. "Sometimes I'd hear his radio on past three in the morning!" "You have brought up another topic. They found Mr. Spedinski wearing a blue t-shirt advertising KJZM's *Only the Lonely* talk show. Mrs. Buttner, did he ever mention this radio show to you, or are familiar with it at all?"

"Bryan, I do not waste my time listening to such trash. That host, Summer Solstice – why, the things that come out her mouth!"

Summer dragged on her cigarette, flicking the ash smartly into a nearby ashtray. "How the hell do you know what comes out of my mouth if you never listen to me," she barked sarcastically at the image on the television.

Mrs. Buttner pursed her lips tightly, looking as if she had been sucking on a lemon. "Downright lewd and perverted language from a lady, and the seductive way that she talks to her callers; well, I can imagine that it works some people into a downright frenzy."

"So, you *have* listened to the show, then?" McMannish clearly reveled in his ah-ha moment.

"Once or twice, I might have accidentally tuned to it while I was searching for my gospel station…"

McMannish pressed a finger to his ear and nodded.

"We need to go back to Julia, whom, I am told, has some breaking news in this case. Julia, what's going on at the scene?"

"Bryan, a man just informed us that someone claiming to have been present when the body was pulled from the water told him that, not only was the deceased wearing a T-shirt advertising Only the Lonely, the T-shirt had been autographed by Summer Solstice herself.

"This case just becomes more baffling, Bryan; vampires, sexy talk show hosts, and a mysterious death - high drama on the riverfront today!"

The reporter turned her attention to the flashing lights behind her.

"It appears that they are loading the body into the ambulance and moving it to the morgue for autopsy." The reporter looked back over her shoulder. A figure draped in white sheeting was loaded into an ambulance.

"Again, the police are saying that they are withholding any comments regarding suspicion of foul play until the autopsy is complete."

"We have to break from this shocking story for a moment," interjected Bryan. "We'll be back with more details as they happen; on KSBT, your source for news that matters."

Summer retrieved her phone - seventeen missed calls! Summer dialed Melody's number.

"What in the hell are we going to do?" Melody barked.

"How in the fuck should I know, Melody? This is some messed up shit. Yesterday was the first day that we distributed those T-shirts. Do you know what this means? I'll tell you what it means. It means that you and I may have been the last people to have seen Bob alive!"

"I think the poor guy up and did himself in. Let's face it, he seemed like a pretty high strung individual," Melody reasoned.

"Maybe. In a weird way, I hope that you're right. But Bob was a Perceiver, just like I am, remember?"

"Oh, right. I remember him saying something about that cute French guy being a …wait a minute, there's something that you're not telling me."

Summer could almost hear the gears clicking into place as Melody attempted to unlock the clues. Shit.

"I'm coming to your place right now. We need to talk - face to face - and I'm not leaving until you spill what I know you are hiding."

***

A buzzer sounded near the elevator.

"Ms. Stone," the doorman's voice implored.

"Yes, Ed, what is it?" Summer sang into the speaker.

"There's a Miss Melody Forthright down here to see you. She says to tell you to let her in right now, and to get her…um…the fuck away from this mob of reporters that are gathering outside of the building. I've been trying to tell everyone that you aren't home, but they just won't go away, Ms. Stone."

"It's okay Ed, let her up - but no one, and I mean no one, else!"

"Alright Ms. Stone, I'll do my best, but they sure are persistent."

Son-of-a-bitch…reporters at her front door! Summer wasn't as terrified of them as she was of Melody. That girl was like the Gestapo when she caught a whiff of a lie. What to reveal to Melody and what not to reveal to Melody was the unanswerable question dogging her mind.

The elevator opened, spewing Melody into the living room. Her magenta-streaked hair lay dripping and plastered to her head like a wet spider. Flopping down on the sofa, she produced a beer from her jacket pocket and popped the cap, offering a second bottle to Summer.

"Get to ditchin'it, girl," she said, taking a long pull on the amber brew.

"Melody, seriously, I don't know what you're getting at. There is nothing to tell." Summer evaded.

"If there is nothing to tell, Summer, then do you mind explaining this?" Melody reached into one of the countless zippers on her camouflage pants, and dangled a silver lighter engraved with Summer's initials.

"Where did you find that? I have been looking all over for it!" She snatched at the lighter, but Melody held it tauntingly just out of reach.

"Take a guess. I found it in the alley under the streetlamp where you and some guy almost did the bone dance on Friday night. It must have fallen from your pocket while your skirt was hiked up over your ears. Don't get me wrong, Summer; I am not judging you, and you know that I don't give a rat's ass who pokes whom; but a man is dead, and you have been sending out some weird vibe that I haven't until just now put together."

"Exactly what are you getting at, Melody? Are you saying that I am somehow mixed up in this man's death?"

"Maybe…perhaps…I don't know. I was hoping that you would give me some answers. We have been friends for a long time. I don't want to pry into your personal life, but at the same time, I can't help being concerned. Summer, please," Melody implored. "Please tell me what is going on. I promise I won't breathe a word of it. I swear." She crossed her heart with a burgundy-painted fingernail.

Her affair with Lucien had been an ever-expanding secret that had grown larger with each passing day. It would be a welcome relief to get it off her chest.

"I don't know where to start," surrendered Summer, lowering herself onto the chair. Breathing deeply, she began. "Do you remember that strange call I took on Friday night - Lucien from Lafayette Square?"

As Melody listened, she related the events of the past two days. When she told her about Lucien, Melody snapped her fingers and raised a hand in victory. "I knew it!" she declared.

All of the details came tumbling out…the nightclub, the absinthe, and the Vicious Ones. Melody listened with rapt attention, her eyes as wide as a landlord's on rent day.

She trusted Melody, and wished now that she had not kept this secret from her. She realized that she didn't deserve a friend such as Melody, and suddenly felt ashamed. When she had finished her story, she waited for Melody's response.

Melody reclined against the back of the couch. Her fingers drummed rapidly on her knee. "Well, I never expected to hear a story like that one! Bram Stoker on ice skates, Summer, this is like a 'Lifetime for Women' movie! I believe you - I really do. I know you. You are normally so level-headed that this just blows my mind."

Now that she had been thinking back, she was incredulous, too. Everything had happened so quickly that she hadn't had time to really consider what was going down. It was as if she was caught in a whirlwind, and spinning too fast to get her bearings.

"My mind is blown too, Mel. One minute I'm Summer Solstice, wise-cracking radio host, and the next thing I know, I'm having hot animal sex with a vampire in a disgusting underpass."

Melody leaned forward, raising a pierced eyebrow. "It was pretty hot, huh," she asked in a conspiratorial tone. Summer leaned forward, nodding her head. "Prison-sex hot!"

Melody fanned herself with her hand, a sly grin lighting up her face. "Hooooly shit," she said softly.

"To tell you the truth, I haven't even taken time to think about all of it until now." Summer rose from her chair and paced the room. "It's as if I've been under a spell, but I *haven't* been under a spell. That's the thing that's so damned alarming." She threw her hands in the air in exasperation.

"I have been aware of, and consenting to, every single moment of it. I am drawn to this guy like a bitch in heat!" Melody flicked at her shoelace with her fingertip. "Well, he *is* ridiculously fucking hot. I mean, who could blame you? No kidding, he should come with a warning label or something."

Summer laughed. "Yeah, Warning: Close proximity to this individual may cause extreme horniness and a sore pussy."

Melody laughed, doubling over, clutching her stomach and stomping her feet on the floor. "Wait...wait...wait!" she howled breathlessly. "Side effects include, but are not limited to: wet panties, throbbing clit, dick-in-mouth syndrome and some women may experience fainting orgasms that are temporary and usually diminish with continued use."

Summer was laughing so hard she had to hold onto the counter to keep from collapsing to the floor. "Stop it, Melody," she begged, crossing her legs tightly. "You're gonna make me piss my pants!"

Summer rested her forehead on the countertop, laughing until the fit played itself out. Melody had slid off of the sofa and rolled on the carpet clutching at her sides.

God, it felt good to release the tension with totally inappropriate hilarity. The air was lighter in the room, as if the laughter had chased away the gloom. Melody crawled to her knees and pulled herself onto the couch.

"Ahhhh," she sighed, indicating that she was back to normal now.

Summer sat down once more in the seat across from her. After a moment, Melody's countenance turned serious.

"All kidding aside Summer, are you in love with this…this…" casting furtive glances around the room, she whispered, "vampire" as if speaking the word aloud might summon a coven of bloodsuckers.

"I don't know," Summer answered offhandedly, with a shrug of her shoulders. "It's kind of too soon to even think about it." She pulled a cigarette from the pack, poising it in the air for a moment as she processed her feelings. "I don't think so," she said uncertainly.

"I'm crushing on him for sure." Summer crossed her legs and lit the cigarette, inhaling a few quick drags before snuffing it. She really needed to quit this habit, but now was definitely not the time.

"Honestly, there are so many things that I dig about him: his looks, his voice, and the way he dresses…the fucking of course," Summer enumerated. Melody took a long pull on her beer, her lips making a popping sound on the rim as she pulled it from her mouth. "Oh yeah, I'd say you are crushing on him big time," she agreed.

Summer could go on and on about Lucien's attributes, but when she thought about him, her thoughts always seemed to turn physical.

"I believe this may be a purely carnal attraction," she concluded. "You know…the lure of the mysterious and forbidden."

"Good enough reason, in my book," Melody concurred, propping her feet on the coffee table.

"On the other hand," Summer countered. "When I am with him, it's like hanging out with an old friend." She picked at the hem of her shirt, absentmindedly. "I am so absolutely," she searched for the right word, "comfortable with him."

Melody cocked an eyebrow. "I don't know if I'd ever feel comfortable around a vampire. Know what I mean," she cautioned.

Why did everyone seem to be warning her away from Lucien? Other than the first night they met, there hadn't been a single inkling, not one smidgen, of danger. She huffed with frustration. "He has a way," she explained, "of putting me instantly at ease. Mel, I totally forget that he is a vampire."

But he was, and always would be a vampire…and capable of things she would rather not think about. "It's complicated," she sighed.

"Hey, stuff happens that no one expects, and before you know it, you are tangled up in all sorts of drama. The question is: Now what?" Melody queried with a lift of her studded eyebrow.

The Peters

Now what indeed!

By the time Summer left for work, the reporters, distracted by flash-flooding reports, had abandoned their vigil outside of the apartment building. To be on the safe side, she ducked out the back entrance.

She'd kept a watchful eye on the news, but the police were not talking, and no one seemed to know much about Robert "Bob" Spedinski. She hoped Lucien would visit her tonight. She needed to hear from him that he had nothing to do with Bob's death. Poor ole Bob certainly fit Lucien's criteria. It sickened her to imagine the possibility, but it *was* a possibility. She wasn't certain that she would believe a denial if she heard one, but she needed to hear his voice and to evaluate the sincerity of it.

Melody greeted Summer before she opened the studio door.

"The Peters want to see us," she whispered ominously.

The Peters were mid-level managers of KJZM that shared the same first name. Peter Moneymaker and his sidekick Peter Needleman were red, white and blue corporate whores, puckering up to kiss company ass if it helped them to climb the ladder of excess.

"This can't be good," mumbled Summer. She anxiously searched her memory for what she could have done that would warrant a sit-down with the Petes. Oh hell, it could be nearly anything. Following the rules wasn't exactly her strong suit.

She whispered nervously to Melody, "They are never in the station this late unless one of them is in the storage room balling their girlfriend of the week." Summer and Melody entered Peter Moneymaker's office, where she saw both Petes seated on the couch.

"Good, Summer, you're here," said Pete. "Please, have a seat, both of you," said the other Pete, motioning to the sofa opposite them. The Petes leaned forward, clasping their hands between their knees in a concerned posture.

"I'm just going to come right to the point," Pete Moneymaker said.

"Pete and I feel it would be best for all concerned if you both took a little sabbatical... just until this thing calms down."

"A sabbatical?" Summer roared. "What you mean is that you are suspending us!"

"No, no, of course not," Pete soothed. "We just feel," the Petes exchanged glances, "that you might be safer if you didn't have to come back and forth to the station late at night."

He smiled broadly, the overhead light glinting off of his porcelain veneers. "And the corporation does not want to handle any more negative publicity regarding your show right now. We have enough trouble with the FCC and the... shall we say..." he rolled his eyes, sighing, "*questionable* language of your advertisers."

"Of course, we will continue to pay your salary and benefits until you are able to return," said Pete number two, with a wave of his hand. "You are our hottest time slot, Summer. Believe me, this has not been an easy decision."

"One more thing," said Pete. "We ask that you not give any interviews during this time. Let our PR people handle this."

Summer couldn't believe her ears. She felt violated, as if they had torn her clothes off and left her sitting naked on their pleather couch. She was a victim too, and they were treating her as if she were guilty of murder.

"What are you going to tell my listeners? That I just fell off of the face of the earth?"

Pete Moneymaker lowered his gaze, anxiously running his fingers over the crease of his trousers. "We, um, we are going to tell them that you checked into rehab."

Indignation bubbled up inside of Summer like a blister in the hot sun. "Rehab!" She leapt from her seat. "Why fucking rehab? I don't have a drug problem - yet. But you two asswipes may force me to find one!"

"We feel - Pete and I both," Pete continued, motioning for her to sit back down. She did, but only barely, perching on the arm of the sofa. "That the public loves it when people with problems seek help. They identify with their faults and failures, so it will probably boost your career in the long run."

Summer pressed her lips tightly together as she tried to control her emotions. She loved her job. Hell, she even kind of loved her listeners... and now she was going to have to live this lie.

"Plus, if we say that you are in rehab," Pete Needleman grinned cheerfully, as if he was just handing her a big bonus check, "the press will go on a wild goose chase searching for the facility you might be in, thereby diverting their attention from our offices and your front door. We see it as a win-win situation." The Petes nodded in unison

"It's only temporary, Summer." Moneymaker consoled.

Her shoulders slumped forward with the weight of defeat. This would destroy her reputation as a straightforward no-bullshit person. There seemed to be nothing she could do about it.

"Only temporary," Pete repeated.

A win-win. Then why did she feel railroaded? There had to be some leverage she could find. This was business after all. She was tired of being bullied. First the Vicious Ones and now this. Righteous indignation galloped through her veins like the Crusaders riding to take Constantinople. Fucking corporate bastards, forcing her to slink around in the shadows!

"You know what," Summer confronted, setting her jaw and waving her finger. "You two Peters can put your little Peter heads together and concoct whatever you see fit, but if I'm going to be forced to hide out so I don't blow your rehab story, I want double my pay, and Melody wants double pay too. Also, the minute they determine this was a suicide, or accident, or catch the dude that whacked him, I am coming back to work, same as before."

Pete looked at Pete. "I think we can agree to those terms."

They seemed anxious to end the meeting and be rid of her. Maybe she hadn't demanded enough. All she really wanted to do was come back to work, however there was no choice but to wait this thing out.

"I guess there's nothing more to be said then," she surmised, standing upright and smoothing the wrinkles from her skirt. "You have my number when you need to reach me. Until then, don't call me - about anything. I want that pay increase put in first thing in the morning, and don't try to get cute about it - this girl plays hardball, boys."

***

Summer flung open the alleyway door. It crashed against the building, bouncing back towards her face. She kicked it. Her eyes searched the alley, hoping to see Lucien lingering in the shadows. She was still angry about her meeting with the Peters, and needed to talk with someone whom she trusted.

Could Lucien be trusted? Oh God, she didn't know anything about anything anymore. Like a ball of yarn rolling down a steep hill, her life seemed to be unraveling before her eyes. Her usually so-certain mind was as confused as a man trying to find a corner in a circular room.

Perhaps Bob's death and Lucien's arrival in her life were simply a coincidence. Perhaps they weren't. She wondered if vampires held any loyalties. Was there honor among blood thieves? Would Lucien betray her by striking so close to home?

A scuffing sound on the pavement broke her train of thought. Suddenly spooked, she mashed out her cigarette, ducked inside and closed the door behind her with a quiet click. She stood in the stairwell, with her ear to door, listening.

It was a cat...or a rat. Sounded too heavy for a rat...and not right for a cat...in fact it didn't sound like an animal at all, unless the animal was wearing shoes. Shoes! Yes, that's what it was! It was the sound made by the smooth bottom of a man's dress shoe skidding on the concrete... sort of a scuff and a clicking sound. She was loath to admit it, but maybe the Peters were right - she could be in danger here. The sense of invincibility she usually carried vanished. She felt as vulnerable as a turtle on an interstate. Where was Lucien and his promise of protection now?

Pressing her forehead against the cool steel of the door, she willed herself to get a grip. This whole business of vampires and dead bodies had made her jumpy. It was only a sound, she told herself, nothing more. She couldn't stay here forever. She had to walk out that door at some point, if for no other reason than to get to her car. With an ear to the door, she listened once more - it was silent as the grave.

Cautiously, she opened the door a crack, one eyeball peeking at the other side. The coast was clear. She slipped out the door and stepped into the alleyway once more. A rat scurried along the road in the distance, his pupils like two tiny lasers glowing in the darkness.

A hand gripped her shoulder. A shrill shriek exploded from Summer's throat, and she jumped nearly three feet in the air as adrenaline careened through her.

"Summer, mon chére...it's alright. It's only me"

Summer doubled over with relief, her hands on her knees as she gasped for air. For a moment she was sure she was a goner.

"Holy shit, Lucien! You scared the hell out of me!" she scolded angrily. Her palms connected with his chest, shoving him backward a step. His hands went up in surrender, his eyes wide with bewilderment.

"Damn it, Lucien!" She stomped her foot. "You've got to stop sneaking up on me like that." She spun on her heels once, shaking out her arms and hands, attempting to release the pounding adrenaline. "How long have you been out here?"

"I only just arrived the moment you opened the door." Lucien defended. His gaze ran the length of her, his nostrils flaring. "I can smell fear coming from your skin. You're frightened of more than my appearance. What is it? Tell me."

"It's nothing. I heard a noise. I spooked, that's all. Would you walk me to my car, Lucien? My legs feel like pudding." "Aren't you doing your show tonight?" he asked.

"No, not tonight, not until the suits tell me I can come back. It's a long story and I could use a stiff drink. But I'm not supposed to be seen in public for a while." "Then I have just the place. You can fill me in while we drive."

The House of Oh-La-La

Summer steered her 1967 Camaro through the city streets, following Lucien's directions. She related the events of the day. When she told him of Bob's death, Lucien appeared genuinely shocked. When she related her conversation with Melody, she expected him to show some sign of displeasure. But he only said he was happy that he was important enough for her to want to tell her friend.

His hair danced around his face, ruffling in the cool breeze as she related the details of her meeting with the Petes. Giving her knee a reassuring squeeze, he told her not to worry; things have a way of working themselves out. He smiled, and said he was selfishly pleased at the turn of events, because now she had more time to spend with him. Summer thought his remark rather sweet, and it did cause her to look on the bright side of the situation.

Careful not to mention her suspicions, or the earlier encounter with the Vicious Ones, she was mindful to block her thought from Lucien's penetrating powers.

His reassurances put her at rest, and her doubts about Lucien faded to a glimmer.

She cruised through the darkened streets, the horizon of the night sky blood-red and bruise-purple. Above her hung a round, white moon. With one eye on the road, she stole sideways glances at Lucien. He wore a black leather coat. A scarlet woolen scarf hung loosely around his neck. How pale his flesh appeared against that dash of red.

The thought flittered through her mind that her fascination with him might be blinding her to danger. The truth was, she didn't care.

Lucien directed her towards Mississippi Avenue in historic Lafayette Square.

Winding through lamp-lit streets, she felt transported back in time.

Lafayette Square served as a living reminder of the flamboyant Victorian era St. Louis. During the prosperous post Civil War years, the area became one of the most fashionable neighborhoods for the well-to-do. The year

1896 brought a massive cyclone which devastated the area, and Lafayette Square experienced an exodus, as residents migrated to other locales. After decades of disrepair, its unique charm and architecture were restored to the grandeur of yesteryear. Once again, Lafayette Square housed the most fashionable citizens of St. Louis. Whenever Summer had the rare occasion to explore the area, she would peer at the golden light that glowed through the wavy hand-blown window glass of the houses, and imagine the people that lived behind the massive, stately doors. Only as she pulled up to a soaring French Second Empire town home, capped with an elegant mansard roof, did she recall that Lucien was from Lafayette Square.

"Welcome to my home," he said. Exiting the car, he strode jauntily to the driver's side, opening the car door for her. The small gesture of chivalry caused her to walk a little taller, as he hooked his arm in hers and led her up the brick steps to the entrance of his home.

Lucien leaned into the heavy double doors, their hinges creaking against his weight. A lavish interior greeted her. Rococo furnishings blazed with hand-rubbed gold leaf finishes. Sumptuous silk upholstery in shades of sapphire and pearl gleamed in the lamplight.

"Lucien, this is amazing! It's like a museum. I'm afraid to sit down on anything." Summer glided her fingers along a gilt table in admiration. Lucien shrugged. "It is mostly old things I have collected along the way," he said offhandedly. "That table, for instance," he pointed at the piece she was favoring. "That I acquired from the Palace of Versailles. Would you like to hear about it, or would it bore you?"

"Are you kidding?" It wasn't just a table - it was a part of Lucien's past, right here for her to see and touch. "I'd love to hear about it."

"Well," he began, "Louis XV had a separate residence erected on the palace grounds called Petite Trianon," he leaned closer and winked, "to house his mistress Madame de Pompadour."

Summer smiled knowingly.

"His successor, Louis the XVI, later gifted the residence to Marie Antoinette, who, as you can guess, was not inclined to keep the trappings of its former occupant." Summer listened in amazement. This was the coolest history lesson, ever! "Once, while visiting the estate, I admired the very table that you are touching. Marie Antoinette bid me to accept it as a gift from her, and ordered that it be delivered to my chateau. Now it sits here."

Summer pulled her hand from the table, awestruck at its history. Holy smokes! Lucien was full of unexpected revelations. "This once belonged to Madame de Pompadour? You knew Marie Antoinette?" He was tossing around these names as if they were Tom, Dick and Harry. No big deal, just some people he used to hang with.

She found it difficult to grasp that Lucien, with his youthful appearance, was actually hundreds of years old. The mere existence of him seemed impossible, yet here he was. Summer wondered at the synchronicity of history. Marie Antoinette was the straw that broke France's back and spurred the Revolution, which in turn was the reason Lucien still lived today to tell about it.

"Yes, I knew Marie Antoinette - socially, not biblically," he emphasized. She was just a child, really, given to whims of fancy which the king indulged at France's expense."

Kings, Queens, and palaces…Mesdames and Messieurs…Summer felt she was quite an insignificant thread in the tapestry of his history.

"My culture is absurdly romantic, obsessed with love in all of its forms. When a Frenchman falls in love, he is inclined to lavish his lover with all manner of eccentricities, adorning her in jewels and fine fashion." Lucien slipped his arm around her waist. Tilting his head to the side, his eyes captured her gaze. "A Frenchman in love is tireless in his ardor. By pleasing his lover, he himself is pleased." The drumming in her head began again, and she felt the sensation of her soul being drawn into his body. What sort of wicked magic did he possess that could seize her so quickly?

If Lucien was aware of the affect he had on her, he didn't show it. He casually inquired, "Would you like to see more?"

Summer blinked, willing her thoughts back to the here and now.

"More? Absolutely…lead on, please."

Lucien toured her around the expansive house. Among the oil paintings, antiques and the heavy brocade draperies, she noticed retractable steel hurricane shutters affixed to windows.

He became aware they had attracted her attention.

"Oh, those," he pointed to the shutters. "The sun cannot kill me any longer, but it does scar. Like other creatures, we vampires are by nature nocturnal. I don't have to sleep through the daylight hours, but it is my nature to." He ran his hand over the grey metal covering the windows.

"These allow me to keep what hours I choose."

"Do you sleep in a…," she tentatively began.

"A bed," he interrupted. "When I sleep, I sleep in a bed."

She had envisioned him sleeping in a dark, underground chamber hidden in the depths of the house, smelling of moist earth and mildew. The knowledge that he slept in a bed comforted her.

"Would you like to see it?"

"If you'd like to show it to me."

She trailed him up the narrow staircase to the second floor landing, and followed the switchback of the railing to a doorway at the end of the hall. Lucien lifted a floorboard along the wall, extracting an old skeleton key. A shudder ran through Summer as her imagination conjured reasons for the secreted key. With a rusty grind, he turned it in the lock and swung the door wide.

She wasn't certain what she would discover on the other side of the old oak door. She peered into the room, feeling uncomfortable at crossing the threshold. It seemed like a violation of his privacy for her to do so.

An ancient Chinese Marriage bed was the centerpiece of the small room. Carved of camphor wood, the bed was roofed, and enclosed on three sides. A set of four stairs led to a keyhole-shaped opening, through which she spied the thickness of a downy feather bed inside. It was the most erotic bed she had ever seen.

"There you go," he said, patting her on the back. "See…no spiders or dripping candelabra…all perfectly normal."

Reality and myth intermingled in her brain, and she wasn't sure what to believe about vampires anymore.

"There's one last place I'd like show you."

He led her to a room on the third floor.

"This is my studio," he announced.

Summer stepped through the small wooden door into a sparsely furnished room with sharply angled ceilings and open rafters. Aged and peeling plaster freckled the brick walls.

A kaleidoscope of oil paint splattered the wide planks of the wooden floor, and a tall blank canvas sat atop an artist's easel. Staged in front of the easel was a Louis XVI fainting couch, thickly tufted in burgundy velvet. A sliver of moonlight illuminated dust motes skittering across the wood of a primitive farm table.

Of all Lucien's finely appointed rooms, Summer loved this one the best. It was comforting in its simplicity. Its rustic, earthy quality recalled a starving artist retreat. She felt she had entered a cozy garret, high above the fields of Provence. There was a sense of safety here…a haven from all that had been happening around her.

"This is my favorite room of the house," informed Lucien.

"Mine too!" she concurred. "You paint, then? What have you done, can I see your works?" Summer implored.

"In my time, everyone with means studied painting." He picked a cloth from the floor, covering the empty canvas with it.

"I haven't painted in a very long time."

Lucien's arms encircled her waist. Summer melted into his embrace, their bodies fitting together like two halves of a whole. In the stillness of the moment, the weight of the day's events descended on her with an avalanche of emotion. She clung tightly to him, wanting to sob her troubles into his chest.

"Stay with me tonight," he urged. "Forget about everything but here and now." He placed a kiss on the crown of her head. "Trust me on this. Our past is no more or less than a memory, and the future is only a figment of our imagination," he said with a grave and dreadful wisdom. "Mortal or immortal, all we ever have is the present moment." He stepped back, grasping her forearms. Pursing his lips, his brow furrowed with disapproval. "Now turn that frown upside down, and say you'll stay."

Any misgivings she had about Lucien fell away like leaves on a winter tree. He held her spellbound, and she adored every minute of it. The affair that had sprung from curiosity was rapidly becoming her obsession.

"Do you even have to ask?" she said. "I wouldn't want to be anywhere else tonight."

"Brilliant!" He exclaimed. "You stay put, and I will go to the kitchen to see what the housekeeper has left in the way of food."

"You have a housekeeper?"

"She thinks that I work nights, and does not dare disturb me while I sleep right under her little pug nose. Poor thing slaves in the kitchen, and she would be so disappointed to know that her hard work goes down the disposal every night." He turned on his heels and exited the room.

Summer listened to the sound of his footfalls on the wooden staircase grow faint. She sat on the velvet couch, running her hands across the plush fabric. The couch was very old. Everything he had in the house was old. In fact, other than the kitchen, she couldn't recall a single modern object. Why would he torture himself with constant reminders of what once was? Summer wondered if she would ever understand this mercurial man.

She reclined on the fainting couch, her ears listening for his return. God, he'd only been gone a few a minutes, and she missed him already. Her eyes roamed the room, wondering what to do in his absence. Then she had an idea.

Guess Who's Coming for Dinner

Returning laden with food and drink, Lucien stopped dead in his tracks. "Mon Dieu!" he exclaimed.

Summer's nude body lay stretched out on its side on the fainting couch. She propped herself on one elbow, using her hand to support her head. Silken waves of hair cascaded to her shoulders, and his mouth watered at the sight of the ripe, golden apples of her breasts. Her skin was the color of amber grain and her mouth red as a sunset. His gaze followed the swell of her hips to the narrow row of blonde curls which beckoned to him from between her legs. Like a compass to North, his cock pointed towards her plump, pink opening.

"You like?" she purred.

"Definitely, most definitely," he said nodding. "I like very much."

"Then wine me, dine me and sixty-nine me," she growled. "Feel free to reverse the order."

This was his kind of woman! His heart drummed in his ears as he hastily placed the platters of food on the table, never once taking his eye off of her.

Lucien unbuckled his belt, snapping it free from his jeans. He intended on giving her everything she wanted tonight and more. He'd give her a fucking she wouldn't soon forget!

Her hand slipped between her legs as he tossed his shirt to the floor.

"You'd better hurry," she moaned. "I'm starting without you."

His hardened cock nudged through the fly of his underwear, straining painfully against the sharp metal teeth of his zipper. Kicking off his boots, he envisioned spreading her legs and burying his face in her pussy… tonguing every inch, every fold, every opening. Desire surged through his cold flesh like a flash flood through a canyon.

He strode to the couch and, standing over her, stepped out of his pants, his cock springing free, swollen and erect. Summer sat upright.

She drank in the sight of him as she might a Michelangelo sculpture. His chest was hairless with hard, flat pectoral muscles tapering into a slim abdomen, rippling with muscular hills and valleys. Between his strong legs, his cock rose like a spire, rigid and robust, flanked by the fruit of his manhood, as round and firm as two figs.

She craved him, craved his touch, craved the weight of his body pressing heavily on hers. Her sex craved the pummeling of his punishing prick.

Lucien gave her a sinister grin.

"So you want to be wined and dined and sixty-nined, do you?"

Before she could answer, he scooped her up into his arms and carried her across the room. "Care to join me for dinner?" he said, dropping her onto the long wooden table.

The drop wasn't more than a few inches and didn't hurt at all, but the abruptness and force of Lucien's actions sent thrills of anticipation through her body.

"What's on the menu?" she asked.

"You are," he replied, grabbing a mound of soft sweet cream butter from a platter with his fingers. It plopped with a gooey splat on her abdomen. It slowly melted into viscous oil as it contacted her sizzling flesh.

Lucien basted the round hills of her breasts, polishing her globes with the velvety grease. His touch was as cool as satin as it slid over her skin. Snake-eye and Slick had nothing on the wonders of this creamy butter. As he fanned his fingers and greased her abdomen with the flat of his hand, she felt as slippery as an eel. Her whole body squirmed in anticipation, her juices trickling from her and soaking the wooden table below.

"What are you doing to me?" she moaned, bending her legs and opening them to his touch. She longed to experience the oily goodness sliding over her tender folds, mingling there with her wetness. She raised her hips in supplication, but Lucien did not comply.

He licked his lips and smiled, revealing the exquisite points of his canines. "I am preparing to eat you," he said. "And a Frenchman always prepares his dish with butter."

Summer startled for a moment, rising up on her elbows at his remark, which seemed to please Lucien immensely. With a hearty laugh, he pressed her shoulders back to the table.

"Relax," he said. "Culinary cunnilingus is what I have in mind. Now just lie back while I show you the two things the French are most skilled in - food and fucking."

Under this circumstance, she didn't mind being the main course. Stretching out on the table, she plucked an apple from the tray. "Only if you promise to make me squeal," she said before popping it whole into her mouth.

Lucien laughed, shaking his head. "No, no," he said, removing the apple. "I have something else in mind to put in there."

"I can see that you do," she replied, hungrily eyeing his erection. Her mouth watered for the taste of it.

She watched Lucien dip his hand into the honey pot withdrawing a sticky glob. Every nerve of her body stood in anticipation as she wondered where he would place those honeyed fingers. He held his fingers a few inches above her lips. She looked up at him, unsure what to do. He opened his mouth, raising his eyebrows in encouragement. She followed suit, opening her mouth like a baby bird, to catch the drops of golden sweetness on the tip of her tongue as they slid from Lucien's fingertips.

With honey still pooled on her tongue, Lucien lowered his mouth onto hers. Summer shared the taste of wild honey with him, swirling her tongue over his and coating his teeth with the sublime nectar, paying special attention to the sharp points of his fangs.

Her whole body suddenly felt light and insubstantial, as if she had no weight at all. She had a strange urge to purposely slice her tongue along the razor sharp tip of his fangs and allow her blood to mingle with the honey. This urge was as compelling as the one that caused her hips to rise and writhe in the direction of his cock.

Any thoughts of danger and death fell away. The want to surrender her blood to him was all consuming, as instinctual and primitive as a mother's need to offer her breast to her hungry baby.

Lucien pulled his mouth from hers, his eyes like a cheetah, startling in their ferocity. Summer shrank with alarm at the feral look of them. Shuddering, he closed his eyelids for a moment, and she heard his voice in her head saying, "Do not test my limits." When his eyes reopened, she was eased to find the golden glow diminished, but it left her with the sense of having made a narrow escape from some terrible danger.

Lucien seemed to have righted himself, because he snatched another dollop from the pot, this time filling her navel with a golden pool of honey. Although it was no more than a teaspoon, she felt the weight of it pressing on her skin. Her abdomen muscles clenched and quivered as his tongue dipped into her navel, lapping at the honey. She rolled her eyes in ecstasy, a moaning laugh rumbling from her throat as she reveled in the sublime joy of the sensation.

"Oh, fuck me now," she pleaded, arching her back against the smoothness of the worn, wooden surface. She had her fill of appetizers and hungered for the main course - a big skewer of hot man-meat.

"You Americans," he chided, walking around the edge of the table until he came to a spot near her head. "Always with your obsession for fast food." "Oooh," she whimpered with the realization that he would be prolonging her head-swimming bliss, as he dipped the head of his cock into the honey pot. Golden nectar flowed in thick rivulets down his granite shaft.

His glistening prick head looked like a piece of hard candy, and she wanted to lap it like a lollipop.

Lucien straddled her, the most delectable hors d'oeuvre she had ever seen inches from her mouth. She rolled his cock in her hands, smearing it with the sticky honey. With long, languorous strokes, she licked his shaft, from the bristly edges of his pubic hair all the way to the tip of the head, where the honeyed goodness lay hidden inside of the small slit.

Lucien groaned in approval, placing his hands behind her head and raising her mouth to his prick. She sucked it in whole, feeling the head glide against the back of her throat. She sucked with joy, working the head between her lips, while her hand rhythmically pumped his thick shaft. Her other hand, wet with honey and saliva, grasped his buttock, feeling the taut contraction of the muscles there, as he gently stroked in and out of her mouth.

Ignoring her own needs, she focused only on giving him pleasure. But the feel of his trembling, the sound of his breath as it caught in his throat, excited her. She pressed her thighs together to quell the throbbing there, and found she was quite literally dripping with desire.

Holding his cock with her hand, she brushed the head over her lips, her tongue snaking out to swirl its circumference teasingly. He looked down at her, the muscles of his jaw strung taut with ecstasy, his hair falling around his face and framing it with a savage luxuriance.

He thrust into her mouth more forcefully now, grinding his quivering cock in slow, circular motions after he sank its full length into her. It quivered and jumped in her mouth, ready to spew forth his passion onto the back of her throat. Summer tipped her head back, her hand on his buttock forcing him deeper. His mouth drew back into a grimace, and she knew he was close, but trying with all of his might not to come.

She loved being the cause of his rapture, and the power she had over him at this moment thrilled her to the bone. Torn between bringing him to orgasm and wanting to save him for herself, she used one hand to pump his engorged shaft with a rapid, staccato rhythm as her other hand slipped between the split of his buttocks, a finger easing into the dark, tight opening there.

He threw his head back, his shoulders trembling. Summer felt his prick swell even larger, and she knew he was going to come. But she wanted his cock for her own and she would not let him orgasm. She drew her mouth from his prick, placing pressure with her thumb on a spot just beneath the swollen head, halting his imminent ejaculation.

"Ahhhhh!" he bellowed, long and tortured, with a timbre that rattled the window panes.

Maintaining the pressure of her thumb on his cock, she smiled inwardly with the knowledge that she planned to torture him to the brink and back, again and again.

Summer dished out her tormenting tease until Lucien was panting and pulling his cock from her lips in protest.

Although he was capable of recovering with remarkable rapidity, he did not want this moment to end. He had her for the whole of the night, and he meant to use the time well. He had fed earlier on a pitiful soul, and blood thirst did not gnaw at his bones. His hunger now was of a different sort.

Summer grinned at his throbbing prick with the satisfaction of the cat that ate the canary, and he returned the grin, with a mind to dish out a little sexual agony of his own.

Pulling the plain wooden chair to the end of the table, he took a seat between her legs. Summer propped up on her elbows watching his movements.

"Come closer," he said, motioning with his fingers.

She wriggled her bottom closer to him.

"A little more."

She pushed nearer.

"Don't be shy," he coaxed. "Bring that pretty little pussy over here." Before she could comply, he grabbed her by the ankles, pulling her bottom to the edge of the table causing her to gasp in surprise.

She was so near now he could smell the heady scent of her musk and see the moisture glisten on the golden strands of her mound like morning dew on a wheat field.

He ran his hands up her silky thighs, from her throat sang a sweet sigh.

"Open your legs for me," he entreated. "Open them and let me see the petals of your flower."

Her knees dropped wide, exposing the luscious blush of her pussy, its delicate form reminding him of the calla lilies in the garden. He longed to be like the hummingbirds and dip his tongue into its cup.

With his fingers, he opened her folds, revealing the budding gem of her clitoris. She gasped, rolling her head from side to side, as he blew a thin stream of air lightly over the tiny button.

Dipping a strawberry into the honey, he tickled her swelling clit with the berry's prickly tip. She squirmed, her hips writhing in retreat and then rising to beg for more. With the deftness of a surgeon, he teased her tiny, throbbing knob, flicking the berry lightly over the very tip, then turning it in tight, slippery circles on the organ, ever careful to apply the right dose of pressure on the sensitive nerves lying just below the skin.

Honey slid into her fleshy folds, coating them with glistening juiciness. Watching the juices run down the edges of her labia, Lucien recalled the long-forgotten taste of strawberries and honey. He sometimes placed food in his mouth just to stir his memory. Often the aroma or the texture of it would cause his mind to conjure the flavors that his condition had dulled over the numberless years.

Lucien put the firm, ripe fruit between his teeth and drew it down her sticky slit, his eyes peering over her mound, because he found the ecstasy on her face to be beautiful and arousing. She arched her neck, bringing her finger to her mouth and biting down on the knuckle in sweet anguish.

How exquisite she was, with her tawny skin shimmering with the buttery coating, her breasts as tempting as Eve's apple. Mesmerized, he gazed longingly at the streams and tributaries of the blue veins in her breast. The slumbering Beast inside of him stirred. He squeezed his eyes, willing it back to sleep. With his tongue, he pushed the honey-drenched strawberry inside of her and then sucked it back into his mouth. She writhed, clutching her breasts, rolling her nipples between her fingers, and his prick ached at the sight of her touching herself.

The aromatic scent of her musk clung to his lips, and he inhaled her desire deeply into his airless lungs. Oh, to be mortal again - to know her taste. How unimaginably wondrous it would be, for a single precious moment to make love to her in the pale light of the morning. But it would be a wish unfulfilled, he knew; a dream just beyond his grasp. Her body trembled as his flattened tongue lapped at the sticky goodness concealed in her secret garden. She panted and moaned, raising her hips from the table, supplicating him to take her.

Now was the time, he decided. Lucien rose from the chair, scraping it across the floor with a dull sound as he nudged it out of his way. As he stood, his anxious cock brushed her pussy, the head nearly dipping into her slippery fissure. A milky drip of cum oozed from his slit and, along with it, his last drop of self-control. He grasped her hips, rolling her onto her stomach. Summer's feet slid to the floor, and she backed her small firm bottom up against his loins. Snatching another handful of soft butter, Lucien greased her flushed cheeks, rubbing the fatty cream in wide circles. Summer arched her back, strutting her fine ass before him like a queen cat.

His appetite had been teased for long enough. He would never be more ready. She would never be more ready.

Lucien buttered his cock, "It is time to feed my starving prick." "Oh holy…Mmmm," she cried, mumbling something unintelligible into the tabletop as Lucien pushed his oily cock into her pussy. Her vagina felt as narrow as the eye of a needle as he squeezed into her tight sheath. She bucked against him, the thick butter making a slurping sound as he worked his prick inside of her. His cock glided smoothly along the satiny surface, and he increased the intensity of his strokes with ease.

Their bodies seemed as one as she rocked in perfect tempo with him. She tossed her hair to one side, and Lucien's gaze hovered over the thick vein that throbbed along the curve of her neck. The Beast growled, low and menacing. Even in this most private of moments it would not let him rest.

He thrust harder, beating the Beast into submission. The rickety table trembled and groaned. Summer stretched her arms out grasping the sides of the table. So fierce was his pounding that he felt himself lifting her off of her feet. The sound of her flesh slapping against the table, and the quiver of her buttocks as he rammed his cock into her nearly drove him to madness. His pace quickened, each penetration punctuated by short grunts that rumbled from his throat. Were they from him or the Beast; he didn't know.

He reached around her hip and rolled a finger over her blossomed clit. The greasy butter mingled with her juice, and Lucien coated her tiny jewel with the slick mixture. It was like a smooth, polished stone beneath his fingertip. She responded to him like no other. Her warm willingness was completely human and such solace for his dark loneliness. Summer squealed and rose up on her tip toes, tilting her pelvis. "I love the way you fuck me, Lucien," she cried, grinding against his loaded cock. Her approval ignited inside of him, spurring him on. He fucked her with complete abandon, jack-hammering his cock into her so ferociously he had to grip her hips lest she buck away.

Summer's legs began to shake. A deep crimson flush crept up her back as her muscles strangled his shaft. Her small, puckered hole winked at him as he watched the blur of his prick invading her pussy. Lucien wet his finger with her juices and pressed it to the opening. Summer did not draw back, but instead entreatingly pushed against him. She wanted penetration in her darkest of places, and he was happy to oblige. Carefully, his finger entered the shadowy tunnel, where he felt the rhythm of his cock in her pussy through the thin strip of flesh. He matched the rhythm, fucking her with both his finger and his cock. Her guttural cries and obscenities echoed through the room as she hurtled towards climax. He felt himself carried along with her orgasm, as her tiny body levitated from the table from the force of it. Her pussy squeezed his prick with a stranglehold. He felt the pull and ripple of her muscles milking his cock, and his whole body trembled and jerked from the force of the orgasmic fluid rocketing through his prick. He clutched her hips, his nails denting her flesh, and with one final, satisfying thrust, he showered her womb with ejaculate.

Awash in a sense of euphoria and bliss, he dreamily rocked against her, his spent, half-hard cock still nestled inside of her. He didn't want to leave her because, for this brief moment, the Beast was still, and Lucien felt nearly alive once more. As a seed that had been planted in the damp spring earth, so was the seed of love planted in his heart, taking root, and stretching to be nurtured by the warm rays of Summer.

Lucien collapsed on top of her, sandwiching her between him and the table. For a long moment, he laid there, filling his lungs with short bursts of air, too spent to move, his cock becoming flaccid and slipping from the warmth of her pussy.

Summer's body began to heave beneath him so that at first he believed she was sobbing, but then he heard chortles of laughter. Lucien rolled off of her, and she turned her body to face him.

"What's so funny?" he asked, knitting his brow.

"Ahhhh, nothing," she sighed, biting at her cheeks to hold back her giggles. "That was just fan-fucking-tastic, that's all," she exclaimed, kicking her legs and laughing.

The bright cadence of her laughter was a light shining brightly in the blackness of his existence, and he adored the sound. With her, he felt unbroken - purged of the curse that oppressed him.

"What's for breakfast?" Summer joked.

"Breakfast? We haven't even gotten to our midnight snack yet!"

After a welcome shower, Lucien led her by the hand to the antique Chinese bed. They crawled through the opening onto the cool sheets. Through the night, they made love - tender and unhurried - in the cozy den of the marriage bed.

Summer drifted to sleep wrapped in the pallid arms of the vampire, Lucien du Charmont.

Summer Solstice – Private Dick

When Summer awoke, she found herself back in her own bed, in her own apartment. Try as she might, she had no recollection of how she had gotten there. The last thing she remembered was drifting off to a dreamless sleep. For a moment, she wondered if last night had ever happened at all, but the satisfaction tingling through the cells of her well-fucked body and the ache between her legs confirmed that it had. The light streaming through her windows cast long shadows in the room, and she knew that it was well past noon. She called out Lucien's name, but was certain he wouldn't answer.

Summer was disappointed to find that he'd gone missing. He had a way of coming and going that was very unsettling. Now that she was alone once more, the misgivings about her relationship with Lucien returned with a vengeance. The affair had taken a direction that she had not anticipated. She had begun to miss him when he wasn't around. She craved his company and his touch. When she wasn't with him, her thoughts were on him. Her growing need for him frightened her. She felt herself pulled deeper and deeper into his life, and found she didn't want to leave. The vampire had her in his control as surely as Renfield had succumbed to Dracula's mesmerizing mind.

This was not a good position for her to be in, she reasoned. Her usual common sense simply flew out the window where Lucien was concerned. Her heart sank like an anchor to the bottom of her stomach when she realized the futility of this relationship. Sure, she could play at this for a little longer, keep telling herself she could walk away anytime she wanted, but at what cost? No matter how she turned it around in her head, it all came down to the fact that he was a vampire - an immortal.

Perhaps the Vicious Ones had it right. This was an impossible and ill-advised situation. At some point, old age and death would creep in like a thief in the night, and steal her away from her vampire lover. She would, one day, just be a distant memory to him, another in a long list of lovers spanning hundreds of years.

Their obvious differences cast a sprawling, dark shadow over her heart.

By the time she had showered and dressed, she knew what she must do.

***

"Good afternoon, Ms. Stone."

"Hiya, Ed," Summer spoke to her doorman through the speaker.

"Ed, I am going to be hanging out in my apartment for a while, sort of a little vacation. I really don't want to be disturbed, so if you would please tell anyone who asks for me that I am out of town. Right now, the only exceptions to that would be Melody, who you already know, and my cousin from Paris who is in town…a tall fellow, long brown hair streaked with blond, handsome, speaks with a French accent. Just those two, no one else, okay?" "Sure thing, Ms. Stone." She could hear him clicking his ballpoint pen as he spoke. "I'll write it in the pass-on book so the other guys know about it too. Have a nice day, Ms. Stone, and I'm sorry to hear about the ruckus over the dead guys." "Thanks, Ed." She released the button and rummaged in her jacket which hung over the back of the chair. *Did he just say dead guys, plural?* Summer thought. *Nah, I probably heard him wrong.* She extracted her cell phone from her jacket pocket. Turning it on, she found sixteen missed calls from Melody with accompanying frantic messages.

I'd better call her. I didn't even say goodbye the other night…just disappeared. She is probably freaking out.

Melody answered on the first ring. "Where the hell have you been? I have been trying to call you for hours! Summer, something terrible is going on." Melody didn't even allow Summer a chance to speak. "Did you know they found two more men floating in the river?"

"What? Two more men?"

"It gets worse—they were both wearing T-shirts that you signed! They are calling these the Eleanor Rigby murders because the corpses are all found wearing 'Only the Lonely' shirts. It's all over the news, haven't you seen it?"

"Actually, Mel, I was with Lucien last night, so, no, I didn't see it. What is happening? None of this makes any sense."

"Perhaps your fanged friend can shed some light on the subject, Summer. Have you given that any thought?" Summer felt quite taken aback by the near-accusation. The Lucien that she knew was not a monster who killed people and dumped them in the river, but Melody's question planted a seed of doubt. Their first night, right here in her apartment, he had acted strangely, in a rush to leave, and then less than forty eight hours later, just steps outside of her building, Bob turned up dead. What was it he had said to her in the vampire club...he fed on only the lonely? Summer didn't want to dwell on what she was thinking. It was too horrid to consider.

"I have, Mel, believe me, I have. I wanted to talk to him about it last night, but one thing led to another, and it just never came up. But, trust me, if I see him tonight I will be damned sure to mention it." "Call if you need anything, Summer. Oh, by the way, the station released an announcement. According to them, you checked into rehab for an addiction to prescription pain medication that started when you had a back injury. So at least they didn't tell everyone you were an alcoholic or a crack head." "Great, just great," Summer grumbled. "I've never had a back injury, but lately I am starting to feel a big pain in my ass. I'll call you tomorrow and let you know how it went with Lucien. Right now I need a hot shower and a stiff drink."

She hung up the phone and poured a double shot of Cutty Sark.

Someone was sending her a message. Of that, she was certain, but who?

She didn't want to consider it, but she had to admit that Lucien was at the top of her list of suspects.

But what could be the motive? She ruled out jealousy, that was absurd, but by his admission, her callers certainly qualified as appropriate entrees. Was she unwittingly leading Lucien to them, she wondered?

In her heart, she refused to believe that it could be true, but love blinded. Perhaps she rejected her suspicion because she viewed it through the veil of her emotions.

The Vicious Ones and their threats made more sense. The murders could be cruel warnings to her, but how did they know where to find her fans?

***

The sun dipped below the horizon; black clouds silhouetted on a purple sky as Summer picked her way through the busy cobblestone streets. Fearing recognition from her new-found notoriety, she had piled her hair up under a fedora, dressed in a sleek black pantsuit, and had hidden her eyes behind shaded lenses. She marched up to the door of Down for the Count. Before she could rap on the heavy steel, the door swung open.

"Good evening, Miss Summer," Gino smiled broadly, flashing his fangs. "If youse is looking for Lucien, miss, he ain't here."

"Thanks, Gino," Summer replied, stepping through the door. "I'm not here looking for him. I was hoping you could tell me where I might find Nitro." She slipped a ten spot into Gino's breast pocket.

"Hmmm," he hummed, peeking at the note in his pocket. "I don't know if I know where he is."

Greedy fucker. "I see. How about Marcus?" She crammed another ten in Gino's pocket.

"I might know where I saw him last… gimme a minute to think."

"Okay," she acquiesced, tiring of this cat and mouse game and waving a fifty under Gino's nose. "Perhaps Mr. Grant will help you remember where I might find Dodger."

Gino snatched the bill from her hand. "Oh, yeah, I just remembered. Da bunch of dem is in da back at their usual table. Want me to show ya?"

"Thanks, Gino, but I think I can find the way. You've been very helpful."

"Anything else I can do fer youse, you just call on Gino, okay miss?"

Yeah, yeah… I'll be frigging bankrupt with the prices you charge for help.

It was early. The bar was hushed. A few patrons huddled in corner booths. A female vampire dined on the wrist of a gothically garbed Donor.

They eyed her with a stare as frosty as a Frigidaire.

Summer scooted past them, and turned a corner. Seated at a round table, she spied the Vicious Ones, laughing and playing quarters with shot glasses. She watched, mildly amused, as Gaston missed an easy shot, and Nitro busted on him, shoving Gaston's shoulder. The chair tipped, spilling Gaston to the floor. They whooped and banged on the table like frat boys.

A bunch of overgrown college kids with more power than brains.

She shook her head reproachfully. Their ass clown behavior buoyed her confidence. She could handle them…piece of cake.

Summer sauntered towards the table, removing her glasses. Their faces sobered. She fixed Gaston with a school-marm stare, and he bashfully picked himself up from the floor and took his seat.

"Mind if I join you?" she inquired, assertively pulling a chair to the table and seating herself to the left of Marcus. The dumbfounded looks on their faces were priceless.

She needed information from these buffoons, and she'd have to grab the upper hand to get it.

"Anyone have a light?" She held a cigarette to her lips. Nitro leapt up, and leaned across the table, fumbling with his Zippo.

Summer pointed to Dodger's drink. "May I?" Dodger opened his mouth to respond, but before he could form the words, she lifted the liquor to her mouth and knocked it back without a shiver. The Vicious Ones exchanged nervous sidelong glances.

Good. Her new-found courage confused them. Possibly, they were wondering if they had underestimated her. Dodger kept peering over her shoulder, as if he expected someone - Lucien perhaps - to walk out of the shadows.

She would make nice and see how far that got her.

"I was hoping you boys could help me." Summer removed her suit jacket, draping it on the back of the chair. She had chosen not to wear a bra, and she knew her breasts played peek-a-boo behind her sheer, flesh-toned blouse. She leaned over, resting her breasts on the table, which she knew caused her cleavage to deepen and swell.

"My eyes are up here, fellows," she chastised, to no avail. No matter how hard they tried, their eyes had a mind of their own and repeatedly drifted down to her breasts. Summer deliberately brushed her forearm against her nipples, creating a distraction as they puckered and hardened.

"Let me explain," she continued. "I suddenly seem to have a problem. Corpses are popping up in the Mississippi like lifeless carp. You boys wouldn't happen to know anything about that, would you?" Summer saw their eyes all shift to Marcus for a response. They obviously took their cues from Marcus. Well, she'd just have to weave her magic on him. She may not have vampiric powers, she reasoned, but she had feminine wiles, and they were just as deadly in the right hands.

"Marcus," she purred, scooting her chair next to his. "Are you the leader of this gang of miscreants?' She placed her hand on his thigh, her skin crawling at the gesture.

"I, uh," he coughed, directing his response to her breasts. "I guess you could say that."

"Oh, goodie," her fingers walked up his thigh. "You can imagine why I might be wondering if you and these handsome young men might know something about this situation, can't you?"

She directed the question to the bristly soul patch on his chin, watching it bounce around as he chewed his bottom lip. He nodded sheepishly.

"I've heard about the bodies," he said. "But I swear we didn't have anything to do with it."

"Well, you did frighten and threaten me the other night, so naturally, I assumed…"

From the corner of her eye, she saw the others exchange furtive glances.

"Threaten? Yeah, I guess we did do that." Marcus fidgeted. "I'm awful thirsty…anyone else thirsty?" he asked to no one in particular. He motioned to the bartender for another round.

Good, his throat was dry. That meant she was getting somewhere.

Summer scrunched up her nose flirtatiously. "You're kind of a big bully, aren't you?" Her hand squeezed his leg as she baby-talked, "Wanna tell me why you were being such a big bully to me? I'm not so bad, am I?"

Marcus resembled a scolded school boy. He began to nervously shake his leg from side to side, his jeans rustling against the top of his boot.

"I'm sorry for that. The community was talking after you showed up here the other night. After all, you are a Perceiver, and that kind of set some nerves on edge. To make it worse, you were with Lucien."

What an odd thing to say, she thought.

"Lucien? How does Lucien make it worse?" Marcus cleared his throat. The tension at the table was palpable. "Lucien is sort of a loner." Marcus explained. "He has this 'history' with females, well, vampire females anyway. I'll just say that he has made the rounds of the local vampginas. But he never sticks around for long, which is no big deal to any of us."

He looked at his friends, shrugging his shoulders and laughing nervously. "I mean who cares who he bones and disowns, right?"

The boys nodded in agreement.

"Yeah, who cares?" echoed Dodger.

"But the women," he continued, his head shaking from side to side, "they never wanna forget him, and that's where the problems come in."

Summer squirmed uncomfortably in her chair. It wasn't easy hearing about Lucien's exploits with other women. She kept reminding herself that they were in the past and had nothing to do with her. Still, the pattern Marcus described was disturbing.

"We all like a little pussy now and then," he grinned. "But when Lucien gets at it first, the girls don't want anything to do with the rest of us. They'd rather sit on their twats for eternity, panting for him to throw some dick their way."

Summer's stomach did a black flip at his remark. Scenes from the previous night flashed before her eyes, and she couldn't help but wonder how many other women he had taken to those heights of passion.

"So, knowing his pattern with women," Marcus leaned back in his chair, his fingers casually playing with a stir stick, "and you being a Perceiver, we could predict where this was headed."

"And where exactly is this headed, in your opinion?" Summer asked curtly.

"Duh," Marcus mocked. "He has his fun, you go all ga-ga over him, he dumps you, and you seek revenge on vampires - a woman scorned and all that."

Well, that answered the question of their threatening attitude towards her. It was so simple; she wondered why she hadn't thought of it herself. The information about Lucien was alarming, but that wasn't why she was here. She had pretty much made up her mind about what she was going to do regarding the matter of Lucien.

"You seem like a smart guy, Marcus." She fished an ice cube from her drink. Holding the ice between her fingers, she sucked on it, making certain that he noticed her tongue playing with the hole in its center. "Do you think that Lucien could have anything to do with my 'problem' that we were discussing earlier?"

"I, uh, I couldn't really say." Marcus evaded.

Summer allowed the ice to slide from her fingers and drop between her cleavage. The boys' eyes were as wide as a twelve year old's looking at his daddy's porn collection, as they watched her fingers fish around for the frozen cube.

God, they were as easily distractible as a pile of puppies. She drew the ice from between her breasts and popped it into her mouth. Nitro's drink slipped from his hand, landing upright on the table with a sloshing thud. He wiped at the spill with his sleeve.

"Anything at all that you might know could really help me out."

Summer wasn't certain if she was pouring it on too thickly. The rising bulge in Marcus' pants confirmed that she had hit at least one of her marks.

"I suppose it's possible that he's involved." Marcus squirmed, attempting to adjust his jeans around his tell-tale boner. "Like I said, Lucien is a loner. I don't know much about his habits, but dumping corpses in the river is not his style." He paused, rubbing his chin thoughtfully. "Nah," he said finally shaking his head, "no way would anyone find his kills unless he wanted them to be found. I don't know if you realize it, but Lucien is an old and powerful vampire."

"Yeah, he's as close to an ancient as we have in this city," Nitro chimed in, a hint of pride in his voice.

"He doesn't need the safety of a group anymore." Marcus sounded almost wistful when he said it.

The awe Lucien's name evoked in them was striking, and she wondered what she truly knew about Lucien. Perhaps they knew him better than she did, or perhaps no one really knew him at all.

"Well, you have been very generous with me tonight." Summer stood, flinging her jacket over one shoulder, her sheer blouse clinging to her breasts like cellophane. "I want to assure you that I am on your side. I do not intend to blow the whistle on vampires, no matter what happens between Lucien and me. You have my word. Do I have your word that you had nothing to do with the murders?" The Vicious Ones nodded in agreement, and she believed them. They were probably too stupid to plan anything so elaborate.

"I guess I'm finished here, then." Summer tossed a hundred dollar bill on the table. "Next round is on me, boys. Have a nice night."

Marcus grabbed her hand, flashing his fangs in a smile, "Why don't you stick around for a while?"

"I'd love to, honey, but I have something I have to do."

Like a Stake through the Heart

Back at the loft, Summer removed her jacket, turned on the television and waited for Lucien.

"Another body was pulled from the river today," the reporter announced. "A man fishing downstream in Jefferson County reeled in an unexpected catch…"

Summer snatched the remote and turned off the TV. It felt as if a tiny dwarf with a pickaxe was mining the veins in her skull. She decided to step into the shower and try to clear her mind.

Of all of the features in her loft, she loved her shower the most. It had cost her dearly, but the glass-enclosed, double-sized unit, with sixteen adjustable full body showerheads, was her favorite spot. She could adjust the spray from a fine rainforest mist all the way up to powerful pummeling jets.

Tonight, she chose to turn the showerheads on full blast. The steam rose, filling the room with a dense vapor. Closing her eyes, she stood on the tiles, allowing the pulsating jets to hammer her weary muscles. The tension dissolved from her body and disappeared in soapy rivulets down the drain. She mentally rehearsed what she was going to say to Lucien, and hoped she had the gut for it.

The thought of him weakened her, and she wondered if her resolve could sustain the sight of him. That is, if she even saw him tonight.

With a sigh of half-hearted conviction, she turned off the shower. The voice of Humphrey Bogart came from beyond the bathroom door. She must have left the TV on, she reasoned. "I was born when you kissed me. I died when you left me. I lived a few weeks while you loved me," she heard Bogie lisp as she towel-dried her hair. She wrapped her body with a towel and stepped through the door into her bedroom, the steam from the bath rushing through the opening in a thick fog.

Through the mist she made out the form of Lucien, lying nude on his stomach across her bed, chin planted into his palms, as he watched television. His boyish ass was as round and white as the moon hanging outside the window.

She found that his sudden appearances no longer stunned her. In fact, she had grown to expect them.

He rolled to face her, propping his head in his hand. His penis lay unapologetically flaccid on his thigh. "You know what?" he chirped as casual-as-you-please. "I believe I like your place better than mine!"

The bottom dropped out of Summer's stomach as she looked at him there, all grinning and lively, knowing that she was about to rain on his parade.

"No, really," he went on, apparently not noticing the distress on her face. "Your place is quite modern. I like it. In fact, I'm thinking of tossing out my old things and getting with the times." He smiled broadly. "What do you think?"

"What do I think?" she repeated, sinking into a chair. Oh, Christ this was going to be even harder than she thought. Why did he have to look so damned happy? She felt like such a heartless bitch. Squaring her shoulders, she took a breath and uttered the four words most feared by men, "We have to talk."

***

Lucien waited impatiently in the living room. His fingers drummed the arm of the chair, his mind raced trying to piece together the source of her concern, but his thoughts came up as empty as his attempts to read her had.

With each moment that he waited for her, a little wire of tension drew within him. Perhaps she was angry because he put her in her own bed last night, but woe to the sleep-vulnerable vampire in the presence of a mortal, no matter how trusted or beautiful she might be. There was more than one way to lose your head over a girl.

At last, she entered the room, her hair wet and sleek, her body swallowed up by the plush white robe that she wore. It reminded him of a butterfly encased in a wooly cocoon, although it was lifetimes ago since he'd seen one.

"Now, what's this about, mon petite?" he asked coaxingly. "Lucien," she began, her arms folded across her chest. "Corpses are being pulled from the river every day. They're multiplying like a school of fish!" His eyes followed her as she paced back and forth across the room.

"Every one of them is wearing an Only the Lonely T-shirt that *I* signed." She turned, fixing him with a basilisk stare. "Don't you find that just a little bit strange, because I sure do."

He pondered what on earth she was getting at, and as two and two began coming together, he didn't like what they were adding up to.

"Twenty-four hours after I meet you, my fans start turning into the dearly departed." She threw her hands into the air, the overgrown sleeves of her robe dropping to her elbows. "I'm sorry, Lucien, but I can no longer ignore the coincidence," she said, adding air quotes to the word "coincidence."

He couldn't believe his own ears. Was he really going to have to defend himself against her silly accusations? She was playing detective, and he was one of the usual suspects. He wasn't shocked, just bitterly disappointed.

"Summer, are you saying that you actually think I have something to do with this?"

She paused, her gaze sweeping some unseen point in the distance.

"Yes, Lucien, I do," she said finally. The notion that she would confront him with this allegation after their night together was as painful as if she'd driven a stake into his heart, and felt just as fatal. Like a cornered cat, Lucien felt his hackles rise.

"Summer, this is ludicrous," his voice bellowed. He sprang to his feet and paced the room. Summer scurried out of his way, perching on a bar stool, her jaw set with determination.

"First of all," he raised a finger to the air, looking directly into her eyes. "Your friend Bob was a Perceiver. Did you know that Perceivers risk their lives every time they are discovered?" "I-I didn't realize…" she trailed off wordlessly, her lips still parted in mid-sentence.

"Some vampires make a sport out of hunting down Perceivers, and Bob just announces it over the airwaves. He might as well have put a sign on his back that said Bite Me." Lucien pumped his fingers mimicking flashing lights.

"What about the others, Lucien?" Summer folded her arms across her chest, her chin raised in challenge. "If you can come up with an explanation, believe me, I would love to hear it."

"Honestly, I don't know about the others. I'm sure that I have fewer clues than the police do." Lucien braced his arms on the back of the sofa, leaning his body in Summer's direction. "Speaking of the police, why don't you stop bumbling around like Inspector Clouseau and allow the police to do their jobs?" he asked, mockingly. The set of her face had rage written all over it as she sprung from her seat as if she'd backed into a cactus.

"The police!" she shrieked, tossing her arms in the air.

He felt her agitation from across the room, and he kept one eye on her hands in case she decided to chuck something at his head.

"I'm supposed to just sit idly by while someone is sending a message that is obviously meant for me? The fucking cops haven't even called to talk to me!" She marched from one end of the room to the other, as the words spit from her mouth. "They are my callers...my T-shirts... and I am the one that is hiding out like some damn low-life criminal."

"I still don't understand what this has to do with me," he pleaded. Didn't she see that she was making the facts fit her conclusion, instead of the other way around?

"You're a vampire, a fucking murderer, for Chrissakes!" The crimson blush on her face was the color of fresh blood. "And you just happened to appear in my life at exactly the time that bodies started to drift to shore."

"I do not murder," Lucien insisted, the insult hotly burning in his chest. "I hunt."

Summer stared wide-eyed with a look of incredulity. "What's the fucking difference?" she asked smartly.

His rage bubbled up like noxious green acid.

"What's the difference, you ask me?" he growled. "Ignorance," he roared at her. "Ignorance is the fucking difference!"

Summer backed into the safety of the armchair, and drew her knees up to her chest. Lucien moved to the window, putting some space between them. He hadn't meant to frighten her. A lump of regret formed in his throat, and he swallowed it down whole. His eyes scanned the darkened waterfront.

The surface of the Mississippi was smooth as glass tonight, reflecting the silvery moon like a mirror. But deep beneath the calm surface, the currents violently twisted and churned...like the Beast within him. Lucien stared out the window, the glass reflected Summer's image, but not his.

"I know humans like to think they are at the top of the food chain," he said quietly. "But what if they are not? What if there is something in the shadow that is stronger, faster, and smarter?" He saw her reflection move as she raised her head, looking at him with narrowed eyes. He turned to face her.

"I am that something," he said, locking his gaze to hers.

She didn't say anything for a moment, and then she replied with pursed lips, "But it's still killing, all the same."

"Yes, I kill - the lion kills, the falcon kills - and I kill!" he cried. "What would you have me do? I - have - no - choice!" he wailed, as he slid to the floor.

She rushed to him, dropping on one knee. Her hair was dry now, soft and wispy, and he wanted to bury his face in the gold of it.

"Try to understand," she cajoled. "If you were me, what would *you* be thinking?"

She would never comprehend. How *could* she comprehend? It was like a guppy trying to understand a shark. He rested the back of his head against the cool window glass, a sigh of frustration hissing from his lungs, like air through a leaking lifeboat.

"For starters," he raised his hands in emphasis, "how about your average, everyday American-made serial killer - has that possibility crossed your mind, or have you just decided that Lucien the vampire is guilty without a trial?"

He searched her eyes for an answer, finding sorrow there and something else. Grief?

"Doesn't what we've shared mean anything to you at all? Have I just been a curious diversion?"

He wasn't certain he wanted to hear the truth, and as he awaited her answer, Dread crept in on silent paws; it kneaded his flesh and then curled into a ball on his chest. Summer turned away, her shoulders jerking up and down as she made small sniffling sounds. Lucien looked on helplessly as she attempted to regain composure. Try as he might, he could not examine her thoughts.

After a moment, she turned to him, her cheeks stained with tears which she hurriedly brushed from her face.

His arms reached to enfold her, to comfort her, but she eluded his grasp, rebuffing his embrace and rising abruptly to her feet, and as she did Dread rose from its slumber. It stretched and yawned, sharpening its claws on his bones.

"There's something else that I need to tell you." She swallowed hard, swiping her tongue across her lips. "I think we have to stop seeing each other, and not just because of the killings." She turned her back to him, and as he sat in the chill of her shadow, Lucien felt the frosty fingers of isolation snatching at him, pulling him into its emptiness.

"I am starting to have feelings for you - genuine, powerful feelings."

Turn to me, he willed, directing the silent request at her mind, but she would not, and Dread kissed him on the mouth, smothering him like a succubus, and thieving the air from his lungs.

"What if I'm falling in love with you?" She walked further from him, and the inches might as well have been miles. With each step, he felt their connection grow weaker.

"Fuck, I've never been in love before. How do I even know if it isn't already happening? What then? You're immortal and I'm…I'm not." The news that she might love him should have brought him joy, but instead it hung over his head by a slender thread like the sword of Damocles, ready to drop at any minute and slice him in two.

"Where does that leave us, Lucien?" She couldn't even look at him.

Here it comes, the inevitable end. He knew it before she even uttered another word. He knew it because he felt all the light go out inside of him, and he reclined there in the darkness of his misery, her words like daggers through his heart.

"I am wishing to hell right now that we had never met, because no matter how this ends, it does have to end."

He crumpled against the wall, her declaration hanging in the air like thick, rolling fog. All he heard was the pounding of his heart in his ears drumming: *too soon…too soon…too soon.*

He desperately searched for the words that would change her mind, wanting to fight for her, not willing to give up.

"Summer, please don't do this," he implored. "Not yet." His heart was full and overflowing with things he wanted to tell her, clinging to a sliver of hope that his words would be enough to bring her rushing into his arms. Finding the strength in his legs, he rose and walked to her. Taking her by the shoulders, he turned her towards him.

"I need you," he entreated. "In my darkest hours you are in my mind like a beacon of light."

He glimpsed his existence without her, replete with endless, aimless nights, feeble candles and dusty books.

"Don't put out the light, Summer," he urged, shaking his head. "You are still young. There is so much more that we can share."

"And for how long, Lucien? A week, a month, or less, like the female vampires you have collected and discarded," she said, her voice dripping with contempt. Lucien's body recoiled as if he'd been blindsided by a sucker punch.

"The female..." he sputtered. "I don't even want to know how you found out about them. But this is different - *you* are different," he protested.

She rolled her eyes in disbelief.

"I know full fucking well," he admitted, "that I should spurn involvement with humans, but I wanted you." He shook her by the shoulders until she looked him in the eye. "I want you still."

She lowered her gaze, shaking her head slowly from side to side.

How she'd found out about his past he couldn't guess. None of it mattered now, but still he felt he needed to try and explain.

"Do you know how cold and unfeeling female vamps can be? They're sometimes more predatory than the males. I don't want them," he protested. "I want you!"

Summer broke from his grasp, turning her back on him once more, as if she didn't care to hear his explanation. Lucien pursued her. She had her say, and he would have his. He stood behind her, wrapping her in his arms, and murmured in her ear.

"For nearly three hundred years I have wandered this earth, drifting from city to city, lover to lover, finally convincing myself that I needed no one, and that no one would ever again need me." Recalling his spent days, he once again felt the numbing crush of desolation.

"Then I heard your voice coming over the radio, and something inside of me moved. For those few hours every night, I would listen to you, and I felt human once more, connected to something. I wanted to experience the warmth and innocence of a human woman, to hold her mortality in my hands."

He felt her muscles relax as she softened against him. His heart leapt, encouraged by this one small sign.

"Mortals are born with the knowledge that someday they must die; when something extraordinary happens in their lives, they cherish it even more because time is fleeting." He laid his cheek atop her head, his breath stirring the filaments of her hair.

"I wanted to be that something extraordinary for you, Summer."

"Oh, Lucien," she sighed, turning to him and burying her face in his chest. "What are we going to do?"

She sounded so forlorn, as if stripped of all hope.

It seemed a weighty anchor dragged his heart to the bottomless sea of remorse. In seeking the redemption of his lonely soul, he had only visited his misery on her. His mind reeled, realizing that she was now as broken as he was. It chilled his bones to think of what he'd done, and the bitter taste of self-loathing rose in his mouth like bile.

"I'm so sorry," he said, his eyes burning with tears he could not cry.

He squeezed her tightly, crushing her to his body. "Believe me, I never meant for it to be this way."

Summer looked into his eyes, her chin quivering. "It's my fault too. I wasn't an innocent bystander. I thought I could handle it, but I just didn't see it coming." She covered her face and wept into her hands.

Lucien knelt on one knee in front of her, the truth of her words pressing heavily on his heart and mind. The affair seemed beautiful and true, but it was as cursed as he was.

When he considered the life he might have doomed her to, his body trembled at the horror of it. He imagined her insecurely examining her aging face in the mirror, as she grew older while he never changed. He thought of the children she would never bear, and he withered with the shame of his selfishness.

He couldn't save his family from the revolutionaries, and he couldn't save Summer from the torment he had personally delivered to her doorstep. He was as ineffectual now as he had been then. Impotent in body and soul, so filled with disgrace he couldn't bear to look in her eyes.

"I have no right to ask for more than I've already taken," he said. Lifting her delicate hand to his lips he kissed it, as he did the first time they had met. "Bonsoir, Mademoiselle."

A suffocating shroud of sorrow descended on Summer as she watched Lucien stumble out the door. The room turned as cold and empty as outer space, and she shivered uncontrollably; not from the chill, but from the earthquake of grief which trembled through her veins and rattled her bones. In the course of a few hours, the affair had ended, but its impact, she knew, would live on. The vampire had changed her life, profoundly and irrevocably, in ways she feared she had yet to discover. Curling inside of her robe, she stared at the moon, hanging high and white in the starless sky, feeling very small and very alone.

Salty tears of anguish flooded her eyes, flowing in remorseful streams over the hills and valleys of her face.

She would never forget him, she knew. Her eyes would never stop searching the darkened streets for a glimpse of him. Her heart would always hold a tender place for him. The beautiful vampire would haunt all the days of her life, and always it would be Lucien... Lucien... forever, Lucien.

Le Louvraie

In the distance, a phone rang. The ringing became louder as she floated back to consciousness. Rubbing her swollen eyes, she answered the phone. "Summer, this is Melody. Can you talk? How'd it go tonight with Lucien?" "Mrrumph...what time is it?" Summer asked, the memories coming back to her, and wondered if it had all been a dream.

"It's a little after two." Two? How long had she slept? She had cried herself to sleep, crumpled on the sofa.

"A.M. or P.M.?" Summer asked.

"Two A.M. Oh, I'm so sorry, Summer, were you sleeping?"

"I guess I was. It's okay, I'm awake now."

"Well, what happened?"

Only the end of my life as I know it.

"It's over, Mel - we're over. I think we both knew it had to be this way." She tried to sound convincing.

"I'm really sorry," Melody consoled. "Are you alright?"

"That remains to be seen," she sighed.

"What about the dead dudes? Any info from him about them?"

"He never actually said that he wasn't responsible, but he never said that he *was* either. I don't know what to think."

"Speaking of thinking, I was wondering, do you remember how many of those T-shirts we handed out that night? It sure seemed like a lot, and what if everyone who got a T-shirt is going to take a float trip down river?" That was a scary thought. Summer remembered signing and signing.

It had been a good turnout.

"Oh shit, Mel, I don't remember how many of them I handed out and to whom." Then she remembered the box. "Holy crap!" she screamed, bounding to her feet. "Melody, I just remembered that contest entry box is still in the backseat of my car!"

"Who gives a shit, Summer? Let the Petes worry about that dumbass contest."

"No, Mel, the box has all the names and addresses of the people who received T-shirts! Oh God, why didn't I think of this sooner? I could have taken it to the police and maybe stopped some of these murders."

She was already throwing on her clothes and shoes as she juggled the cell phone. She grabbed her keys and took the elevator to the parking garage.

"Come on! Come on!" she bitched at the elevator for its slow descent.

Finally, it groaned to a stop, and the doors slid open.

With Melody still on the line, she raced across the garage floor to her car.

"Melody, I am going to take this box straight to the police, but first I want to see how many names are in there." Summer unlocked the car and opened the back door.

The box was still on the floorboard. "Okay, here it is." She paused a moment after opening it.

"Melody, something's wrong. There's nothing in the box. It's emp…"

Something crushed the back of her head. A searing heat split through her skull. Summer's eyelids fluttered, she toppled forward into the back seat, and then the lights went out.

***

A laser of white hot pain penetrated the inky depths of unconsciousness, shredding Summer's brain. She tried lifting her head. Everything seemed upside down. She felt weightless and uncoordinated. *Open your eyes, Summer*, she willed. *Open... your…eyes.*

Her eyelids squinted forming two small slits; peering through the blur, the landscape looked foreign and surreal. Trying to blink the haze from her vision, she turned her neck to look around, and a lightning bolt of pain pierced her skull.

Above her, the low menace of growling rumbled in her ears. Everything was topsy-turvy. Up was down and down was up. She tried to wipe her eyes, but her arms were unresponsive, hanging limply over her head.

"Finally, you're awake."

The voice came from down by her feet…up by her feet…her disorientation was so complete, that she wasn't sure which direction was which.

"I was beginning to worry that I had killed you before I could murder you."

Swallowing the throbbing pain in her head and neck, Summer lifted her head to the direction of the voice.

"Hiya Summer! It's me, Jerry. Do you remember me now?"

Jerry leered down at her. Between his feet, she saw legs tied with rope and suspended from what appeared in the moonlight to be a large tree branch. Her eyes opened wide in terror. They were *her* legs!

"Oh, hey there Summer, can I help you with anything today?" Jerry play-acted. "Oh sure, Jerry, just be a good little sycophant and clean things up around here, and when you're done with that, how about you kiss my pretty ass too." He mimicked her voice and inflections.

"Well guess what, Summer? I know what color underwear you're wearing right now, because I have a bird's eye view of your cunny from here." Jerry rounded his fingers to his eyes like binoculars.

She tried to lift her head, but it felt like a forty pound pumpkin on a Popsicle stick.

"Oooh, I can see your perky little tits, too. Too bad, I'm gonna be the last person to ever see them. I want you to know that they are real soft. Do you moisturize?"

What was going on? She felt she was in a dream from which she could not awaken.

"Jerry," she said, her words slurring as she tried to form them. She wondered if she had suffered a stroke. The words took so long to go from her throbbing brain to her mouth. "What... are...you... doing?"

"Oh, now you're interested in what I am doing! You were never interested before."

She tried again to move her arms, but they dangled above her head like a marionette.

"If I had known that hanging you by your feet above a wolf enclosure at the fucking zoo was going to be the thing that got your attention, I would have done that a long time ago."

Summer dropped her head back trying to see the scene below her. Pairs of yellow eyes stared back at her. Undulating shapes, blacker than the shadows, weaved like strands of a living knot as they paced in tight circles below. Lips, red as blood, curled into snarls revealing rows of thick, white teeth. Summer gazed into the face of death and screamed, or tried to—she didn't have air in her lungs and couldn't force it up her throat. Her eyes scanned for a means of escape, but the only way out was down into the den.

"First, I'm gonna tell you what I've done. Then I'm going to tell you what I am going to do. And you, Summer Solstice…well, I guess that *you* are just going to have to hang around and listen to *me* talk for once."

Had she died and gone to hell? Was this her punishment for loving a soulless vampire?

"Jerry, don't…" "I thought I told you to shut the fuck up, Summer!" he bellowed. "I want to tell you what I have done for us, and you are going to shut your big fat flip mouth and listen!"

Summer closed her mouth. She burned with loathing for the little troll, but she had no choice but to do as he said.

"First, I took out that creep, Bob - no particular reason - just something about him that I didn't like. I think it was when I saw him whispering in your ear, talking dirty to you at that kinky boutique, and you smiled."

"No, Jerry, he wasn't talking dirty -"

"Summer, shut the fuck up!" Jerry roared.

A fearsome growl arose from the wolf pack.

"I talk, you listen; that's how this is gonna work," he commanded, fixing her with an insane glare.

"Or I cut you loose right now, and you are a big piece of Summer jerky for those wolves. I hold the talking stick now, you got that?"

Her ankle joints tore with the weight of her body; the pain like rusty nails.

"I want to thank you for allowing me to take that contest box to your car. Those names and addresses made it so fucking easy to find those losers. I could tell that those ass-clown callers bored you, Summer. People who are that fucking boring should be drowned at birth."

She heard the soft padding of feet as the wolves ominously assembled below her. She saw the movement of dark shapes, but her eyes were going dim, and it was like looking through gelatin.

"Then that French guy called you, and I could tell that you *weren't* bored with him. What if he started to call you every night like I did? Where would that leave me?"

Jerry's body tilted slightly off balance shaking the branch. Summer swung like a pendulum. There was that pumpkin head feeling again. Jerry just kept talking and talking. Why wouldn't he stop?

"So, I decide right then that I had to get rid of him. You see, I know what that guy is, and you know what that guy is. I wish ole Frenchy wasn't what he is, because it would have been a lot easier for me. If croissant-dick had been a human, I could have just thrown his ass in the river." The blood rushing to her head was pushing her back into darkness.

Jerry's words trailed off in the distance.

"Don't fall asleep, Summer!" Jerry barked. The pack fidgeted beneath her, an occasional low growl rumbled through the shadows. "Not when I'm just getting to the good part. Don't you want to hear my motive? Everyone wants to know the motive! Even the freaking damn wolves want to know my motive!"

Summer opened her eyes, willing herself into consciousness. She tried to assemble Jerry's ramblings into coherence, but her brain wasn't working right. Everything was muddy and thick, as if the events crawled through a muck-filled swamp, and by the time they seeped into her tortured brain, they were distorted and unrecognizable.

"It really was a great plan. I started knocking off guys right and left because I wanted to keep that French fuck away from you for good. I actually put the lights out on all of those guys in one night, but the fatter ones floated to the surface faster than the pencil necks, so they just kept finding them, day after day. That part I fucked up. I wanted them all found at the same time. I wanted to make a statement."

Summer could see his eyes darting crazily as he revealed his sick-ass, diabolical plan.

"I knew they would cancel your show. Then that fucker couldn't call you anymore, and I would have you all to myself. But you started fucking that fucker, and well, I just can't have that. You have to die. Just like those other loser assholes, Summer, you are too stupid to live." The light of the moon glinted off of the long, curved blade of a knife that Jerry brandished in his hand.

Terror filled her lungs, invading all the spaces where air should be. Her chest felt like a million balloons straining against a net.

"I mean, who in their right mind fucks a vampire? That's just sick."

He screwed up his face in disgust, spitting a glob of foamy saliva from his lips.

"I am very disappointed in you," he chastised, shaking his head with disapproval.

"Vampires are extremely predatory creatures. Take it from me, I know. He was only going to use you up and then throw you away anyway, Summer. I'm doing you a favor. At least I am going to kill you all at once, not piece by piece like he will."

A gust of wind whistled through the tree, shaking the branch to and fro. Summer's body jerked on the rope. This was it. She was going to die at the hands of this maniac; she knew it! Her whole body trembled uncontrollably, tears sliding from the corners of her eyes and plopping to the ground below.

Jerry stumbled, nearly dropping the knife. Righting himself, he declared, "Alright, enough fucking chit-chat! This time Summer, *I'm* going to be the one to disconnect *you*!"

Jerry raised the knife. The wolves whined. The black clouds parted, unveiling a sliver of moonlight. A shadow emerged from the rustling leaves and a hand grasped Jerry's raised arm, the moonlight illuminating his scarred and punctured wrist.

A Donor...Jerry was a Donor!

She wasn't certain if she was dead or alive; if this was reality or a dream. It was Lucien, silhouetted against the moonlight like a dark angel.

The wolves bawled

"Etre silencieux!" Lucien commanded.

The pack cowered.

Summer observed what followed as if watching a macabre stage play from the wings.

Lucian lifted Jerry to his feet, holding him in the air with one arm. Jerry's scream pierced the night. An ear splitting crack sounded. The branch gave away. She fell to the ground with a thud, fire ripping through her back. The ground vibrated as a second body slammed down. The snarl of beasts rose above the sound of tearing flesh. The smell of blood filled the air. A lone wolf charged for her neck.

"Arrêtez vous, le fils d'une chienne!" Lucien's voice reverberated in the bloody enclosure.

The wolf skidded to a stop. Summer felt his rancid breath on her face. His lips curled as a low growl thundered up his throat.

"Allez vous faire foutre, avant que je vous casse le cou," Lucien threatened. Tucking its tail, the wolf slunk into the darkness, emitting a high whine.

A bolt of white hot lightning ripped through her spine, a metallic taste filled her mouth. Her eyelids fluttered. The shadows turned to twilight, the twilight to inky blackness, and then no pain.

Picking up the Pieces

In the days which followed, Summer drifted in and out of consciousness. Life-sustaining fluids flowed into her wrecked body through a tangle of tubes. Sometimes, at night, she thought she'd see Lucien standing vigil at her bedside. But when she asked the nurse if she, too, had seen him, the nurse would shake her head and slow the flow of the morphine drip. The blood black bruising gradually turned to blue, then brown, and by the time it had faded to a sickly yellow, Summer was able to stay alert most hours of the day.

Through a haze of narcotics, Summer related the events of that horrific night to a police detective, omitting the part about Lucien. Although the detective grilled her for an answer, she insisted she could not recall who had extracted her from the wolf enclosure and delivered her to the hospital door.

Days turned to weeks, and weeks to months. Summer's scars healed, but her legs were stubborn. The fall from the tree had fractured her spine.

With time and the grace of God, the doctors advised, she might regain mobility.

The grace of God...God saved no grace for her. Just as His face had turned from Lucien all those many years ago, He had turned from her for loving him. Summer's heart felt as crippled as her body.

One wintry morning, the physician informed Summer that she could be discharged from the hospital to convalesce at home, but that her present condition required someone to care for her until she was able to walk.

Her release from the hospital was a double-edged sword. Summer yearned to be away from the confinement, but she was virtually helpless - a cripple. She had no relatives to rely on. What was to become of her? She had nothing and no one.

Late that afternoon, small snowflakes drifted outside the window of her hospital room as the sun retired for a winter's nap. Melody bounced into the room, bearing the latest Hollywood gossip magazines and a tempting greasy cheeseburger for Summer. At the same time, Summer's physician peeked in to see if she had arranged for her scheduled release the following morning.

She'd been looking to this day with equal degrees of anticipation and dread. Definitely, she wanted to leave the hospital, but where she'd go, she didn't know. Dr. Silver stood at the foot of her bed; the thick folder of her medical records tucked under one arm. The scent of his aftershave wafted fragrant spice through the air. He was short in stature, with thick, black hair slicked neatly into place. Summer liked his lively blue eyes and quick broad smile. As always, a Star of David hung on a gold chain around his neck.

Summer appreciated his manner, which was neither tender nor brusque, but frank in a way that meted out the facts in manageable doses.

"Do you have any relatives that you can stay with on a long-term basis?" he inquired.

Summer shook her head. She was a product of the foster care system. When she had turned eighteen, the magical age when the system yanks away the safety net, she had been on her own. She might as well have dropped to earth from another planet.

"What about your friend here?" he inquired, indicating Melody.

"I'd love for Summer to stay with me, but I only have a lumpy futon that I share with my two cats. It's a third floor walkup, and my landlord's an asshole that won't even install a smoke alarm, much less a wheelchair lift."

Dr. Silver drew a deep breath and squeezed her toes through the sheet.

"I'm afraid, Summer, that if you cannot find someone to stay with you, we will have to release you to a long-term care facility until you regain the skills that you need to care for yourself properly," he cautioned.

Summer turned her face from him, staring at the tile on the wall while tears flooded her eyes. His words and their implications frightened her.

Her tears were a mixture of that fear and sorrow of knowing that she was alone in this world - crippled and alone.

A nursing home! What if she never walked again? She'd live out her years amid the reek of urine and the death rattles of the elderly. A dark despondence settled on her, like a vulture perched on her shoulder. Summer wished she *had* died in that wolf enclosure.

A familiar voice beamed like a beacon in the darkest of hours. "She can stay with me." Lucien strode into the room, taking his place at Summer's bedside. For the first time in many months, Summer felt the light return to her eyes.

"And you are?" the doctor queried.

"I am..."

"My cousin," Summer interjected. "He's my cousin..." The doctor's brow knitted in confusion. "...from Paris," Summer concluded.

"That's right," Lucien confirmed, placing a kiss on her forehead. "I am studying at the university, and my dear cousin is welcome to stay with me. She will be coming home with me tomorrow, if Miss Melody does not mind picking her up from the hospital in the morning. I have a schedule conflict that I cannot change, and will not be available at the time of her release. That is, if that is agreeable with dear cousin Summer."

Summer felt as buoyant as a beach ball. In an instant, everything she'd lost had been returned to her. If Lucien had charged in on a snow white steed, he couldn't have appeared more of a hero. Her dark angel had come to rescue her in her hour of need, just as he had so many long months before. She looked at him - his eyes changed colors like shattered glass, and she felt safe for the first time in months. She knew she'd been under the protection of her pale knight all along.

***

The next morning when Melody wheeled her into the Lafayette Square house, Summer discovered that Lucien had already prepared a bedroom for her, complete with a spectacular view of the park. The Chinese marriage bed, thick with down coverlets and puffs of feather pillows awaited her. She settled into its sheltered comfort, and there she passed the long weeks of her recuperation.

Through the abbreviated daylight hours of winter, Lucien's housekeeper, Louise, tended to Summer's needs. Melody proved to be a true and faithful friend, stopping in daily to cheer Summer with gossip; often bringing her favorite treats and transporting her to physical therapy and doctor appointments. When Summer's doctor refused to refill her pain-numbing morphine prescription, Melody scored some medical-grade marijuana to ease the constant anguish in Summer's shattered spine.

When the sun slept, Lucien settled by Summer's side: watching movies, telling stories and playing games. He schooled her in Bezique, an old French card game, and she taught him the strategy of penny-a-point gin rummy. He surprised her one day, by bringing her jazz collection from her house, so she could listen to her beloved music.

Not a single word passed between them about their broken affair. Lucien was cautious in his affection towards Summer, often slipping her hand into his or stroking her hair, but nothing more.

Oftentimes, as she slept, he would sit by her bedside in the darkened room listening to her breathing, and, as he sat, memories rose and sank in his brain like waking dreams.

A car would pass by, and he would remember a carriage carving through the white snow, its passenger as pale as the silvery moonlight on the drifts. Like pages of a book, he turned these memories one by one in his mind, as one might a beautiful and intricate bauble.

As his mind meandered through the old streets and older shadows of the past, a gradual change occurred in him. He had mourned his lost humanity for too long, he'd decided. Too many precious years he'd filled to the brim with guilt and regret.

A barstool philosopher had once said to him, "Buddy-O, you're either the piss-er or the pissed-on, and every day of your life you gotta wake up and ask yourself -which one am I gonna be today?"

So, when he felt the clarion call, he would leap on the back of the wind - the thrill of flight excited him still -and travel to places far from the city - wretched, dark places that only the brave or the foolish dare go. There he would choose his victim, and, when he was done, both he and society were better for it.

No longer did he have such specific requirements. No, instead he decided to embrace his nature with a new-found gusto, choosing less discriminately, but only taking what he needed and never from the innocent. He would do what he must and let God sort them out in the end.

As time passed, Summer's legs improved, and she could walk for short distances with the assistance of braces and steel crutches. The pain in her spine too often sent her hobbling back to the comfort of her bed.

The sight of her agony ripped at Lucien's heart. She tried to remain cheerful in his presence, but Lucien noticed her retreating into silent contemplation when she thought he wasn't looking. Her mind had remained blocked to his probing since the terrible event, but he could smell her despair - like dashes of pungent curry.

From her bed, Summer saw the long nights of winter shorten, as the pale green of spring pushed its way through the damp earth.

Pain was her constant companion. There was little improvement in her weakening limbs. The doctor issued a bleak prognosis for a full recovery. The limited mobility she had now, he'd said, was the best she could expect.

The prognosis devastated her in mind and spirit. At first she denied it, emotionally turning her back, crossing her arms, and refusing to believe it to be true. She would come through this, she determinedly told herself, and remake her life better than ever.

But in the face of ever-mounting pain and disability, she abandoned the hope of regaining her life as it once was, and a parasitic, wicked anger rooted inside of her, lashing out at everything and everyone. She was furious with Jerry for what he'd done to her, furious with the gods for allowing it to happen. She was even furious with the children who played on the street in front of the house, simply because they could walk, skip, and run. But mostly she was furious with herself, certain that she was at fault somehow. She despised her condition. She believed Lucien had taken her in with the expectation that she would one day return to full health. Now she felt he was trapped by obligation, giving his life over to caring for her.

In the unending hours that she spent in bed, Summer bargained with the universe. If only her health were restored, she'd do things differently. She'd be kinder and more considerate. She'd cherish each moment of every day - and she'd love Lucien exactly as he was, with all of her heart, for as long as he wanted her. But still no miracle materialized.

She suffered through the dark hours when Lucien lay still as a stone in her bed as she feigned sleep. His body so near, yet their hearts separated by a chasm that was both deep and wide.

Her mounting depression caused her to retreat more and more from him. She withdrew into isolation. She longed for things to be the way they were before her injuries. But how could he want her now, scarred and broken, bitter and lost?

Only Lucien had power enough to pick up the pieces of her shattered life and bring her back to wholeness. Twice before he'd come to her rescue. She needed him once more.

Outside, the rain poured down in silvery sheets. Thunder rumbled somewhere faraway. Summer lay sleepless in bed, listening to the rain beating against the windows like machine-gun fire. Lucien spooned behind her, his breath rustling the strands of her hair. She knew he would not go out tonight - too difficult to find what he needed in this downpour. Lately he'd seemed changed…more at peace. The old ennui had disappeared. His eyes no longer seemed as haunted. Behind those prismatic orbs, she detected a new vigor, a bold and magnetic confidence.

She knew from the vortex of energy preceding him, when he had returned home from the hunt, even before he walked into the room. It shamed her how much she coveted his vitality.

Brilliant talons of blue lightning split the sky, the rain so fierce now even the light from street lamps were no more than dim pinpricks. The room was as black as pitch, and it seemed the darkness would swallow her whole. In that tomb-like blackness, she felt the stirring of her heart. She had to seize the moment before it slipped away…before she slipped away, retreating into her small, little world, and locking him out forever.

"My guardian angel," she whispered, her voice no more than a sigh as she slipped her trembling hand into his. She clutched his hand to her mouth, and reaching out to him, she poured out all the gratitude and longing which filled her heart, raining a dozen kisses into his palm, and murmuring with each kiss, "I love you…I love you…I love you…"

Thunder rolled in the distance; a gathering storm.

Lucien bundled her tenderly in his arms, and Summer felt the emotional divide that had separated them close as seamlessly as the blackened sky had sealed after the lightning.

She turned in his arms, reveling in the press of his body against hers. Lingering in the moment, her nose nuzzling into the curve of his neck, the pulse of his artery drummed against her cheek. His fingers stroked her hair with a gentleness that ached.

Holding her head in his hands, he brushed her mouth with his, his lips still full and lush as she remembered. She wanted to smother him with her mouth and play her tongue over his, but she was afraid.

There was only the hush of their breath and the ringing of the rain on the windows. In the inky blackness, her hand found the nape of his neck, and she entwined the tendrils of his hair around her fingers; they slipped through her fingertips like running water.

His body moved against her, and she fit her leg between his, feeling the swell of his manhood on her thigh. A shudder rippled through her flesh, and then a quickening in her loins. She was afraid, but only just. The darkness would hide her scars.

She guided Lucien's hand under her chemise; cupping her hand over his she placed it on her breast. The touch of him was ecstasy and even sweeter than before, because she loved him.

Torrents of rain crashed against the window panes. In the blackness she murmured, "Make love to me."

His voice came low and husky, like dried corn stalks in the breeze, "I'm afraid," he said.

"I won't break," she promised. "I trust you." And she did. She trusted him with her body. She trusted him with her heart. They were both his for the taking, if he still wanted them.

The butter-cream soft flesh of her breast pressed against his hand, its little rosebud blossoming in the hollow of his palm. Lucien's fingers trembled with equal parts fear and desire. For months, he'd only memories of her body to live on, memories so overwhelming he would sometimes take them to a private place behind a locked door where he might relieve himself of them for a while.

Now she lay next to him, her thoughts open and rushing at him like a flash flood. In those thoughts, he saw a yearning for caresses long denied, and desire for pleasures too long ignored…and something else… something secreted in the recesses of her mind…a phantom of a thought, ducking and hiding from his probing like a frightened child.

Her body moved next to him in the blackened room, frail as a fledging bird in his arms.

"Lucien," she whimpered, her knee nuzzling his half-hard cock.

He moved his hips forward, relishing the pressure of her thigh against his rising prick, and he heard himself moan.

Beneath her gown, he filled his hand with the milky flesh of her breast. The lovely weight of it bounced lightly in his palm.

I can do this, Lucien thought. He would make love to her just as tenderly and skillfully as he delivered death's embrace to those who were worthy of his tenderness. No pain. No fear. Only ecstasy. *Yes, I can do this.*

Summer clutched tightly to Lucien's shoulder at a sudden, terrible sound. Blinding arcs of ghostly green, like sizzling Tesla coils, illuminated the night sky as lightning struck a transformer, plunging the neighborhood into a total blackout. Lucien held her closely as they watched the final sparks spit and fizzle to the ground.

It didn't seem possible, but the room was blacker than before. Even with Lucien's extraordinary night vision, he could barely see his hand in front of his face.

"Why don't I light some candles?" Lucien suggested, with a squeeze to Summer's shoulder.

"Don't," she protested, a note of panic in her voice.

"Mon chére, I want to see you."

"Don't be so sure," she replied.

It was a bittersweet heartache to think that the woman who once lay naked across his couch in a fully-lit room was now afraid of a candle's feeble light. It had been too long since Lucien had truly seen her. He wanted to savor the golden wheat of her hair, the swell of her breasts, the curve of her hips, and the slash of crimson between her legs.

"Just one small candle, then," he pleaded. "For me?"

"Just one," she agreed.

He crossed the room, fumbling in the dark for the box of matches he knew lay on the nightstand. He heard the rustle of the blankets as she shifted her body on them and a sound like the tinkle of glass wind chimes as her hair fell round her shoulders. The drumming of her heart he heard clearest of all.

He struck the match against the box and lowered the flame to a single candle. Lucien watched the flame flash quickly in the darkness, and then settle onto the wick, rocking back and forth. The bronze glow threw shadows that leaned and jumped, lapping at the walls as if they were a living thing.

He turned to see Summer sitting atop the rumpled bed. The meager light shone through her thin cotton gown, making it nearly translucent. Her areolas, the color of bruised peaches, peeked through the cloth. So delicate did she appear to him, he felt the need to move at a snail's pace and speak not at all, lest she shatter.

Tenderly, Lucien gathered up the hem of her white chemise. She raised her arms so he might slip it over her head, which he did, and it billowed to the ground as it fell from his hands.

Her long confinement had paled her skin's tawny hue. Her complexion, now cool and blue-white, reminded Lucien of milk in a porcelain saucer.

The lusty curves of her body were angular now...her waist so nipped he could hold it between his hands. Her breasts were as round and lovely as ever he remembered.

She was changed, yes, but in her waif-like frailty, she possessed an ethereal beauty as unearthly as...one of his own kind.

She patted the blankets, inviting him to join her, the corners of her mouth turning with a sweet smile.

He heard the beating of her heart quicken and felt her gaze sweep over him as he removed his clothing, leaving them in a crumple on the floor beside her gown. He stretched out on the cool of the coverlet, and she came to him, sliding over his body, resting her head in the crook of his arm.

Her flesh on his was like a baptism. Her body seemed a holy thing to worship, and he bowed in reverence over it, showering upon it an adulation of tender kisses. Her touch anointed him, her fingers caressing his arms...his shoulders...his face.

"My angel," she sighed, guiding his head to that hallowed altar between her thighs, her musky incense rising from the catacomb of her cathedral.

Never had he known pleasure this sublime. His very cells seemed awash with a transcendent radiance. He put his mouth to that sweet, sanctified place, and there he took his communion.

His tongue lapped the juice spilling from her chalice, and she rewarded him with a tremble and a moan. He sucked her tiny spire between his lips, polishing it with his tongue. She writhed beneath him, and he'd have been content to worship at her holy hall forever, pleasuring her with his mouth. But she pulled him toward her, and he kissed her, his jaws still wet with her musky wine which she sucked from his lips. She filled his mouth with her tongue, and he tasted her again.

He hovered over her, his arms supporting his weight, fearful she might break if laid his weight on her. She stroked his hair, and he gazed into her eyes.

Her legs moved beneath him, and she opened them, inviting him in. He longed to enter but wasn't certain he should.

"Are you sure?" he asked, still fearful of hurting her.

"Yes," she said. "I trust you."

Lucien sat on his heels, bringing her with him, her weight as light as dandelion fluff in his arms. He held her there for a moment, her legs around his hips. His fingers traced the scars on her back, and he wished he had the power to heal them by touch alone.

The storm had passed. He heard the soft plop of raindrops falling from freshly sprouted leaves, as he gently lifted Summer's hips and slowly lowered her onto him. Her arms trembled about his neck as he ever-so-carefully entered her.

The sensation was exquisite, like sliding into warm honey, and she must have felt it too, he thought, because she buried her face in his neck and released a long, sweet sigh.

She clung to him, rocking slowly up and down on his shaft. He helped by holding her round the hips and lifting her to the pace she set. He only supported her while she rode him, he didn't thrust. This moment wasn't for him. Her breath came faster now, even though the strokes grew ever slower.

The sway of her body was beautiful as she undulated against him - gently rolling waves of bones and flesh. Her perspiration, like flecks of mica, shimmered on her skin in the flickering candlelight.

She sank deeper, taking more of him in, her breath coming in short, dry gasps. He knew she was close because she was so wet that every stroke made a soggy, sucking sound. He tried his utmost not to thrust, but he was close too, and it was damn near torture. He wanted to roll her on her back and pound it out, but he couldn't - he wouldn't.

Her body started to quake, and he felt it vibrate deep down inside of her--all the way to his cock. His legs trembled as his climax rumbled like an active volcano. His fingers found her clitoris, making rapid little circles on it to help her get there. Shuddering, she lowered herself onto the full length of his cock. The cries of her orgasm sounding like a choir of cherubs, her tight pussy milked his organ. He felt the charge of his ejaculate advancing up his shaft and pounding down the door like a battering ram. He couldn't help it. He thrust, but just once, and he came like fucking Mount Vesuvius.

Thy Eternal Summer Shall not Fade

The pain attacked her with a vengeance, as if to say, *Stupid Girl, did you think a little pleasure could keep me away? This is my house, and you'll have to die before I leave it!*

The bed wasn't a bed anymore, but little goblins with thumbtack shoes playing kickball on her back. Only the ball wasn't a ball, it was a spiny sea urchin.

Lucien held his hand out, his palm filled with pills. "Here, take these," he said, his face creased with worry.

She could almost hear the pain laughing at that handful of powerless little pills. Nothing had power over it now. Pain reigned supreme.

"They don't work," Summer said, pushing his hand away; a few pills bouncing from his palm and rolling onto the floor.

"I don't know what to do for you," he said, sitting on the bed so gingerly she barely felt the mattress move.

"I think I'd feel better sitting up. Would you carry me to the chair?"

He scooped her up, cradling her in his arms, and, even though his steps were light, each one was like a cigarette burn to her spine.

Pillows, footstool, fussing with blankets, all of this just to be able to fucking sit down, she thought. She was so *over* it.

Lucien sat opposite her, looking like he just hit somebody's grandma with a car. She felt as if she was the one who'd urged him to mow the old gal down.

"It's not your fault," she said. "The pain's always bad. It's just worse now because..." her words trailed off. No sense in saying it; they both knew why it was worse.

"It can't happen again, you know." It wasn't an admonishment, just a statement. She knew what he really meant was not to ask him again, cause it wasn't gonna happen.

One more thing she couldn't do anymore.

"It's late," he said, weariness weaving through his voice. "You should try and get some sleep."

Sleep was a commodity that didn't come easily these days. She'd trade all her money for a few hours' sleep – that is if she *had* any money – which she didn't. The hospital bills had taken everything. If it wasn't for Social Security Disability, she wouldn't even be able to afford an aspirin. Lucien tucked the blanket all around her, making sure she was good and snug. Then he kissed her forehead. It was when he moved to leave that desperation caused her to act. Seizing him by the arm, she uttered only two words.

"Turn me."

He looked at her, the muscles of his face drawn tight, and his eyes searching to and fro as if he hadn't heard her right.

"Don't make me say it again," she pleaded, and she could tell by the soberness of his facial expression that he saw the seriousness in hers too.

He turned and pulled his chair close to her, sinking into it and gazing at her with a quiet earnestness, his hand thoughtfully stroking his chin.

"What you're asking," he said softly, "is a difficult decision for me. I'm not certain I can…comply."

She opened her mouth to voice the thousand reasons she had prepared, but he raised his hand, bidding her to wait. Biting her lip, she waited, her heart like a bass drum throbbing in her throat.

"This is a serious matter, irreversibly serious," he said. "I need to know some things from you, and I need for you to know some things as well." He crossed one leg over the other, sitting back in the wingback chair, his hands resting on the arms, appearing for all intents and purposes like a Mafia Don holding court. "Only then will I be able to make my decision. Do you understand?"

He gazed at her, his eyes the color of indigo, his face the picture of calm composure.

Summer hadn't imagined it would be this way. She'd prepared for angry outbursts and vehement refusals. She'd never expected Lucien would be so…civilized. It was with a mixture of shock and gratitude that she nodded her head. "I understand," she said.

"Tell me," he said, leaning forward, his hands pressed in prayer position. "Why do you ask this?"

She lowered her eyes, gazing blankly at the pattern of the quilt on her lap. "So many reasons," she said. "I am so lost in this pain that I can't even find myself any longer." Her chin quivered, and she felt the promise of tears burn her eyes. "I will never be well, I know that. My injuries have made me a useless, dependant lump of flesh." She raised her eyes, fixing them on his. "Vampires aren't the only thing that can suck the life out of you."

His eyes flashed - a moment of understanding, perhaps?

"Every damn day I grow more bitter, more withdrawn. I hate that I am dependant. I hate that I am crippled, and I hate that I have no purpose," she cried, all the emotions she'd bottled bubbling to the surface in a rush of release.

Lucien, her silent confessor, remained as still as the night. If she were to burden him with ending her mortal life, she knew she must trust him with the darkest secrets of her soul.

"Like a slow leak of air from a tire, I can feel the life oozing from my body…and my heart," she acknowledged. "I don't know which will take me first."

His face was as unreadable as Mona Lisa's smile. All she could do was tell him what was in her heart and hope he would comprehend and grant her request.

"Night after night I see you sit by my side in this damned room, when you should be out enjoying the world. Do you know how guilty that makes me feel?" It was those words, above all others, which broke the dam of tears behind her eyes. She covered her face, wailing the grief into her hands in a torrent of choking sobs.

"Oh, my love," he said, his voice mournful as a coyote bay.

"I love you too much," she cried, the words strangling her tightened throat, "to see you imprisoned by me."

Sniffling, she stroked his hair, the act calming her somehow.

"Lucien," she murmured, "give us both our freedom."

Placing a kiss on her hand, Lucien rose from his chair. Pacing the room, his thoughts turned in his mind.

Her request had blindsided him - but only because he'd considered the very thing himself. Lately, when he'd come into her room, the scent of damp earth filled the air. He knew she was dying. He knew that before the first snowflake of winter fell, he would put her in the ground - his lifeless heart buried in the coffin alongside her corpse.

Yet still, he could not bring himself to change her. It was not his choice to make. If...and it was a colossal "if"...he decided to do this thing, he wanted her to choose this life with a better understanding of it than had been afforded to him. Only then, would he make up his mind. He could not allow his own selfishness to influence his decision.

"I know that was difficult for you, mon petite." He stood behind her chair, his hands cupping the curve of her shoulders. "Thank you for opening yourself up to me."

Her hand patted his. "Thank you for listening," she said. "I suppose there's not much more I have to say."

The slow tick-tock of the mantel clock drummed a reminder in his ear that there were fewer than two hours to perform the conversion - if he were to perform the conversion. There was so much yet to say. "Summer," he began, "there is more to this life than you know. I can't begin to prepare you emotionally, but what I can give you is awareness, and only you can know if it's still what you want."

"I'm ready to listen," she acknowledged. "I'll promise I'll try to keep quiet." The corners of her mouth turned up in a smile, his heart melting at the sight of it.

"Let's get the elephant in the room out of the way first," he said mostly to himself. "Taking life to maintain your own...this would seem like the most troublesome issue, but it isn't." Turning to the window, he looked out upon the dampened landscape. "In fact you will find it remarkably easy."

He recalled his own first time, the hunger, the thirst, so blindingly demanding. "Hours after the kill you will feel something akin to remorse... only lasting until the next feeding when the cycle begins once more."

The rustle of her blankets caused Lucien to glance in her direction, their eyes meeting; he detected no note of revulsion in them. Her blue orbs gleamed with intent interest.

"I promise you," he winked, "after only a few months, it will feel no different than what killing a mouse in a trap feels for you now."

He thought he saw her cheeks dimple with a glimmer of a grin.

"I caution you to never take it lightly, though," he warned, sending a stern look in her direction. "As a neophyte you will need to feed every night - you'll go mad if you don't - and by the time a year has passed, you will have piled up enough corpses to fill a small concert hall."

Her eyes glazed over a bit, looking more inward than out it seemed.

"It's not as glamorous as you've been led to believe. Vampires are opportunistic hunters. For the most part, we are bottom feeders. Our kills are the kind that won't be noticed."

Thankfully, he thought, the world provided an unending supply of thieves, addicts, whores, drunks, runaways, and the occasional organized crime member.

"Now, onto other matters," he crossed the room, leaving the subject behind. "If you think that your life will become less complicated, you couldn't be more mistaken. There are more practicalities than you could dream of."

Taking the seat opposite her, he gathered his thoughts. "I'll try to get through these as quickly as possible," he said, the chime of the clock hastening his speech.

"First, there are three ways to die for good." Recalling the causes, he ticked them off on his fingers as he spoke. "First, the sun…as a young one you must avoid it at all costs unless you want to spontaneously combust, which provides a nice spectacle for humans, but serves no purpose for you. Number two." He held up two fingers. "Beheading… rare but a favorite method of vampire hunters…"

"Number three, stakes!" she added, her head tilting to one side.

He laughed. "Stakes are bullshit."

"What's the third then?"

"Fire…a very unpleasant way to go…it was how my Maker met his end."

The mention of his Maker caused Lucien to recall that he would be her Maker; they would be forever bound together, no matter what may occur. He would always be able to locate her, and to read her thoughts. Unlike so many Makers he'd known, who created and then left the poor creature to figure things out on their own, he did not take this responsibility lightly. If he brought himself to do this, he would carefully train her, educate her in the art of the hunt, take her to the secret places where she could learn from the ancient texts and give her opportunities not afforded to him. His blood warmed at the idea, but then chilled to ice when he realized the thoughts he entertained.

"When I sleep," she said, her voice uncharacteristically timid, "will it be as if I'm…?"

Lucien looked at the sunken hollows, as dark as coal mines, encircling her eyes. Perhaps she yearned for the dreamless sleeping most of all.

"No, my dear," he replied with a reassuring pat on her knee. "Sleep is more like hibernation. You are aware of sounds, smells, movements in your environment, but your powers are weak and your reflexes as slow as molasses in January."

"Oh," she merely said, her facial muscles softening.

Leaning back in the chair, he searched his mind for other things she needed to know. Mentally gathering the list, he recited it to her in no particular order.

"Money - you'll need lots of it," he said, "but not so much you'll be noticed…no private jets, no purchasing whole islands. You'll need it for things like bribes and frequent relocation, because you will never spend many years in the same place."

It seemed a banal thing to discuss at a time like this, but he'd seen what happened to his kind when they failed to plan well, living in basements of foreclosed properties, sharing an old crypt with its skeletal occupant, wearing the rumpled and blood stained clothing stolen off the backs of their kills. It was all too uncivilized for his taste. Investments accrued astoundingly over hundreds of years. He was grateful to have many homes in many places. It made life so much easier. The thought of this made him think of another topic.

"Travel." he said. "Very difficult nowadays with all the added security, impossible to predict flight delays and such, and travel by ship over moving water is used now only as a last resort."

She furrowed her brow. "Why?" she asked.

"Vampires are nearly helpless when in moving water and should you be thrown in the drink, you won't die, but lie at the bottom of the sea waiting for a miracle."

"I had no idea," she mumbled, nervously picking at her fingernails.

"My point is," he continued, "pick a continent and learn to like it, because you may be stuck there a long time."

"There's so much I never thought of," she said, her eyes wide with either wonder or apprehension; he could not tell which.

"Changing your mind?"

"No," she denied shaking her head. "No, only a little overwhelmed."

"There are a few more things I'd like to touch on. What you will need to know as you go along could fill volumes. I want you to be aware of these few basic things because, in a hundred years or so when you come shrieking at me for having done this to you - and believe me you will ..." Her mouth opened in protest, but he cut her off before the first syllable. "I will be of clear conscious that you were alerted to the major downsides of the choice you were so eager to make."

She clamped her mouth shut, nodding her head in acknowledgement. Her legs shifted beneath the blanket, her face drawing into a grimace of pain. Lucien felt his face mimic hers, empathetically experiencing the phantom pain in his spine as well.

Taking her hand, he entwined her fingers with his. "Finally, I want you to know that I love you with all of my heart, but eternity is long. As your Maker we will always be connected, but there will come a time when we part, if only to come together again for a while."

"I would never leave you," she said gripping his hand tightly.

"Well," he said, "vampires do not make the best company. Certain things become part of the DNA, it seems. We become vain, selfish and narcissistic."

"I already am all of those things," she joked, her eyes crinkling with a smile.

"Perhaps," he nodded. "Perhaps you are."

He hadn't nearly covered it all, when the clock on the mantle reminded him of the quickening of time.

"So, there you have it." he concluded. "If you can manage these things, as well as the knowledge that you will live to see every mortal you hold dear put into the ground, and still you truly want this, you are free to make your final argument to me, and I will have to decide if I can oblige."

She lowered her gaze, remaining as still and quiet as the moon in the sky. Lucien clenched and unclenched his fists, not certain what he should do if she hadn't changed her mind.

The transformation had been a curse to him, to others it was a gift. He had no way of predicting how it would be for her - it was different for each. If God existed, he thought, then He surely possessed a heart blacker than his own, for how else could He so cavalierly churn out legions of mortals into the fickle hand of fate, when the decision to make only one of *his* kind was an agony of conscience.

His sense of obligation urged him to grant her request. It was because of him that she found herself in this condition, and it was because of her he had learned to love unselfishly, and finally come to peace with his fate. But was it enough to steady his wrist at her mouth and urge her to drink?

Finally, raising her eyes she spoke.

"Lucien, you once beseeched a man for death, and he denied you. I am asking you to give me life! I beg you; if you truly love me, show me the mercy which was not shown to you!"

Epilogue

"Hello darkness, my old friend. I've come to talk with you again. You're listening to KJZM late night talk radio, and I'm your host, Summer Solstice, and this is: Only the Lonely. I want to thank all of my listeners for their warm and generous support over the past months. I also want all of the lost souls out there to know that you are not alone. Take heart and cling to hope. The hour is always darkest just before the dawn. When you least expect it, your life can change forever. I am so pleased to be back on the air at KJZM in St. Louis. I am completely healed and walking faster and farther than ever before. In fact, sometimes it feels more like flying."

Summer flashed a wink at Melody. "Starting tonight, Only the Lonely will air at a new time. You can tune into the show between the hours of midnight and four-twenty a.m., when we close the lid on another day.

"I would like to dedicate my first show to the man who was instrumental in the salvation of my body and my heart. Lucien, if you're listening, I love you, babe. Keep dinner warm for me. I'll be home before you know it.

"I see that all of the phone lines are lit, and we'll be taking your calls, but first a word from our sponsor: Rusty Trombone's Jazz Lounge; this weekend featuring the live music of Buster Hymen and the Penetrators."

The end

About the author

Susan Gabriel is a writer of paranormal romance novels. She is a proud alumnus of Wilson College for Women.

Susan is inspired to write stories that will spark the imagination of the reader and deliver the message that love knows no limitations, only possibilities.

Susan lives with her husband, her youngest daughter and things that go bump in the night in magnificent Denver, Colorado. She sleeps with a light on.

Also by Susan Gabriel

The Stir of Echo

A gifted, but untrained clairaudient with a secret desire to be dominated is about to find out the truth behind the old adage, "Be careful what you wish for, because you just might get it." Echo Sullivan has all but given up on herself, her gift, and on men, until she meets her charming new neighbor, Flynn. An invitation to his Halloween Fantasy Ball sends her on a course of discovery, and sexual awakening with life-altering choices. Flynn's rakish good looks, sharp wit, and smooth Irish brogue appear to be just what the doctor ordered. He possesses an unsettling ability to recognize, and illuminate Echo's deepest desires; to stir them up and bring them bubbling to the surface. But Flynn harbors a strange and extraordinary secret. What would you say if someone offered you the world...but asked for your soul?

Latest titles from Black Velvet Seductions

Their Lady Gloriana by Starla Kaye
Cowboys in Charge by Starla Kaye
Holly's Big Bad Santa by Starla Kaye
Her Cowboy's Way by Starla Kaye
The Love She Wants by Mila Winters
Punished by Richard Savage, Nadia Nautalia & Starla Kaye
Accidental Affair by Leslie McKelvey
Right Place, Right Time by Leslie McKelvey
Her Sister's Keeper by Leslie McKelvey
Playing for Keeps by Glenda Horsfall
Playing By His Rules by Glenda Horsfall
Sympathy Dance by Sue McConnell
The White Spider of Savignac by V. L. Smith
The Stir of Echo by Susan Gabriel
Rally Fever by Crea Jones

See more of our titles at
www.blackvelvetseductions.com

Our titles are available from:
Amazon
Smashwords
LuLu
Nook
and other retailers

Find Black Velvet Seductions on Facebook
And follow BVS Books on Twitter

www.ingramcontent.com/pod-product-compliance
Lightning Source LLC
Chambersburg PA
CBHW051839170626
46807CB00003B/1262